Penguin Books
Fergus

Brian Moore was born in Belfast in 1921,
emigrated to Canada in 1948, and now lives in
the United States with his wife. His first novel,
The Lonely Passion of Judith Hearne, was
published in 1955 and immediately acclaimed.
This was followed by *The Feast of Lupercal* (1956),
The Luck of Ginger Coffey (1960) – which has also
been filmed – *An Answer from Limbo* (1962), *The
Emperor of Ice-Cream* (1965), *I am Mary Dunne*
(1968), *The Revolution Script* (1972), *Catholics*
(1972; winner of the W. H. Smith Award, 1973),
The Great Victorian Collection (1975; winner of
the James Tait Black Memorial Prize) and *The
Doctor's Wife* (1976). Among the honours Brian
Moore has received are a Guggenheim
Fellowship, an award from the U.S. National
Institute of Arts and Letters, a Canada Council
Fellowship, the Author's Club of Great Britain
First Novel Award, and the Governor General of
Canada's Award for Fiction.

Brian Moore

Fergus

Penguin Books

Penguin Books Ltd, Harmondsworth,
Middlesex, England
Penguin Books, 625 Madison Avenue, New York,
New York 10022, U.S.A.
Penguin Books Australia Ltd, Ringwood,
Victoria, Australia
Penguin Books Canada Ltd, 2801 John Street,
Markham, Ontario, Canada L3R 1B4
Penguin Books (N.Z.) Ltd, 182–190 Wairau Road,
Auckland 10, New Zealand

First published in the United States of America by
Holt, Rinehart and Winston 1970
First published in Canada by McClelland and Stewart
Limited 1970
First published in Great Britain by Jonathan Cape 1971
Published in Penguin Books 1977
This edition published in the United States of America by
arrangement with Holt, Rinehart and Winston

Lines from 'The Auroras of Autumn' by Wallace Stevens,
copyright 1948 by Wallace Stevens, from *The Collected Poems
of Wallace Stevens* are reprinted by permission of
Alfred A. Knopf, Inc., and Faber and Faber Ltd

Lines from 'An Ecologue for Christmas' from *The Collected
Poems of Louis MacNeice* are reprinted by permission of
Oxford University Press and Faber and Faber Ltd

Lines from 'The Waste Land' by T. S. Eliot are reprinted by
permission of Harcourt Brace Jovanovich, Inc., and
Faber and Faber Ltd

Made and printed in Great Britain by
Hazell Watson & Viney Ltd, Aylesbury, Bucks
Set in Monotype Times

For Jean, again

We were as Danes in Denmark all day long and
knew each other well, hale-hearted landsmen, for
whom the outlandish was another day of the
week, queerer than Sunday . . .

WALLACE STEVENS, *The Auroras of Autumn*

When his girl left, Fergus wept. He hadn't been talking about her specifically, he'd just wanted to discuss the situation. But she got up and went into the bathroom, where she kept her clothes. When she came out she wore a sweater and a very short skirt and had tied a schoolgirl bow in her long red hair. He knew he was too old for her. She avoided his eye.

'Dani?' he called, but, deaf to him, she went out of the bedroom. He heard her walk along the brick-tiled corridor, open the front door, and bang it shut. He thought of getting up, going out and apologizing. But then heard the engine of her Volkswagen accelerate as she turned the car into the driveway and drove up to Pacific Coast Highway. In the silence that followed, he got out of bed, walked along the corridor, and went into the living-room. He opened the glass doors and stepped out onto the terrace overlooking the sea. He stood facing the deserted beach and the waves breaking over it. And wept.

After a little time he turned away from the sea, went back into the living-room, and sat down on an orange armchair. Opposite him was a large yellow sofa, and above the sofa a picture window gave a view of the high bare mountains at the rear of the house. Morning sun faded the gay Mexican colours of the room. Behind him, waves slammed on the beach, monotonous as a banging door.

In the bottle-brush tree outside the picture window an unseen bird began to sing. Fergus took a piece of Kleenex from his pyjama pocket, wiped his eyes, then blew his nose. When he had finished, he looked across the room. His father was sitting on the yellow sofa.

His father was dressed as Fergus remembered him. He wore a suit of heavy tweed, the colour of milk chocolate. His silk tie, in the green and red stripes of St Michan's Old Boys Association, was knotted large and lax in the gate of his white, starched collar. His rimless pince-nez spectacles were fitted firmly on the bridge of his nose, the right eyepiece attached to a black silk ribbon which looped over his ear and was draped around his neck. His shoes were brown.

Fergus was afraid. He looked away as a child looks away when it sees something which upsets it. Then, uneasily, he looked back at the yellow sofa. His father was still there.

'Jesus Christ!' Fergus said.

At mention of the Holy Name, Fergus's father began to make the Sign of the Cross, touching, in turn, his forehead, his chest, his left shoulder, then his right, just as he had done in life, even, to Fergus's embarrassment, doing it in public in the street or on a bus, if he happened to pass by a Catholic church. When he had completed the Sign of the Cross, Fergus's father exhaled sadly, his breath riffling the uneven fringes of his heavy, nicotine-stained moustache. His father looked at Fergus with hurt eyes. It was a look Fergus had not forgotten in twenty-one years, and now, seeing it again, he avoided it by getting up and going into the guest bathroom, which was just off the living room. He shut and bolted the bathroom door, went to the washbasin, and examined his face in the mirror. His eyes looked normal: there wasn't even a trace of his recent tears. Certainly there was nothing in his face to indicate that he had just hallucinated or, perhaps, experienced some form of extra-sensory perception. Yet I *saw* him, Fergus told his mirror self. I saw him as clearly as if he were still alive; his skin, that high colour, his breathing, everything. It was like one of those miracles *he* used to believe in, like Lourdes, or the Virgin Mary appearing to Thérèse of Lisieux. Now I know how, after a hallucination, people are convinced that they did see God or some saint. It was extraordinary. I must phone her and tell her. Never mind the row. As soon as she gets to her office, I'll call her.

But then he remembered that his father had been sitting right beside the telephone. Apprehensive, he unbolted the bathroom door and looked out into the living room. There was no one on the yellow sofa. The vision had vanished.

In that moment Fergus felt a sense of loss. How like his father to appear, then disappear again without giving him a chance to say a word. That had been his father's style right up to his final vanishing trick, the night of his sudden death in the downstairs bedroom in Hampden Street in Belfast, his father's heartbeat stopping at the precise moment that Fergus, all unknowing, had begun to masturbate in his own bed, one floor above. So when his mother called upstairs for Fergus to come, Fergus had just come (in his pyjamas) and must delay his rescue dash until he had changed his pyjama pants. Jesus Christ!

Fergus did not say this 'Jesus Christ' aloud, but to his surprise found himself bobbing his head in reverence at thought of the Holy Name. Yesterday he could have said or thought 'Jesus Christ' a hundred times and it would have been a meaningless expletive. But now he was conscious of having taken the Holy Name in vain. Which used to be a mortal (or was it venial?) sin.

Philosophical about it all (the past is the past), he turned towards the glass doors, and there, as always, was the sea, the long Pacific breakers beginning their run two hundred yards from shore. *Thalassa, Thalassa, the loud resounding sea, our great mother, Thalassa.* Although Fergus knew no Greek, he liked to say these words over to himself: he had a weakness for sonorous syllables. Now he said aloud 'Thalassa! Thalassa!' and in that moment saw his father again. His father sat in one of the two wicker egg chairs which were suspended on chains from the terrace beams. His father swung slowly to and fro in the egg chair like an old child on a swing. His father did not look at Fergus. He looked at the sea. His feet did not touch the ground as he sat, slack, in the egg chair.

Fergus slid open the glass doors and went out onto the terrace. Still, his father did not see him. Dignified yet dowdy in his old-fashioned clothes, his spectacles glinting opaque as he drifted towards the sun, turning in a slow semicircle in the egg chair; somehow, the fact that his father had picked this ridiculous place to sit enraged Fergus. The terrace was sixty feet long, and there were other, more suitable chairs. But as he watched his father swing in that silly seat, saw his father's brown shoes dangling inches above the red brick floor, Fergus warned himself to be calm. This time he did not want his father to vanish.

'Daddy?'

His father looked at him incuriously, then looked back at the sea. It was a look Fergus remembered from his childhood. Grown-ups heard you but didn't heed you. They did not have to.

'Daddy, it's Fergus.'

This time, his father did not even look at Fergus; the egg chair turned like a weathervane, swinging him in a half-circle, then, as its support chain ravelled, the chair swung in a half-circle in the opposite direction. His father took from his side pocket a familiar yellow cardboard package: twenty Wills' Gold Flake cigarettes. He placed a Gold Flake in the very centre of his lips, letting it dangle, lighting it with a silver cigarette lighter shaped like a bullet. Many years ago his father had removed a hunter's bullet, lodged beneath a child's heart. The parents claimed the bullet from him as a souvenir, and a month later presented him with a silver cigarette lighter, a larger replica of the bullet. It was inscribed: *To Dr James Fadden with gratitude from Tim Byrne's parents.* Now, swinging in a half-circle in the egg chair, Dr Fadden returned the lighter to his waistcoat pocket and, inhaling deeply, puffed on the cigarette until the tip reddened like a live coal. The inhalation produced a fit of coughing, but Dr Fadden did not remove the cigarette from his lips. The coughing caused a small stick of ash to spill on his waistcoat. He ignored the ash.

As his father's coughing subsided, someone else coughed once, sycophantically, as though agreeing with Dr Fadden's irritated throat. Fergus, turning in the direction of the sound, saw his mother sitting at the far end of the terrace on the steps which led down to the beach. His mother was fingering the small, rubbery, banana-shaped creepers known as ice plant, which covered the bank leading down to the sand. She seemed surprised by the look and feel of the ice plant. She wore a flowered dress, one she had often used for housework, and when she saw Fergus looking at her she crinkled up the skin at the corners of her eyes and smiled as though trying to placate him. It was a smile he had become all too familiar with in her last years, when, financially dependent on him, she had sought to reverse their roles, herself becoming his child. Now, caught in her look and ashamed at his memory of it, he turned from her and hurried back into the living room, closing and locking the glass doors to keep his mother out. He went to the yellow sofa and picked up the phone receiver, reassured momentarily by the familiar dial tone. He did not know why he had picked up the phone. There was no point in dialling for help. *Operator, send the police. I have ghosts in the house.* They would send men with a straitjacket if they sent anyone at all. As he stood with the receiver to his ear, he got the idea that his mother had come up behind him and, guilty, jammed the receiver back on its hook. But there was no one else in the room. The glass doors remained locked. Outside, on the terrace, he saw the egg chair, now empty, turning slowly on its chain. He went to the doors and looked up and down the terrace, inspecting the path to the beach, the bank of ice plants, the bougainvillea bushes which hid a derelict children's playhouse. There was no one in sight.

He turned from this view and sat down in the orange armchair, exactly where he had been when these visions began. He thought again of phoning Dani but reflected that even Dani might not believe that, although he had been seeing apparitions, he was still in his right mind.

Of course, he might not be in his right mind. He did not dismiss that possibility.

A car: he heard it turn in off the highway and stop up there at the top of the drive. It was not her Volkswagen. He rose, stooping so that he would not be seen from the window, hurried down the brick-tiled corridor to the bedroom, stripped off his pyjamas, and put on shirt and slacks. He slipped his feet into loafers, then went furtively into the workroom, put a sheet of paper into the electric portable, and sat at the typewriter pretending to work. He wondered if they had sent someone out to check on him: perhaps a private detective? But even as he considered it, he knew it was not true; they weren't even thinking of him. Redshields had not phoned in three weeks. Boweri was through with him.

The doorbell rang. Ding-dong! No one ever came down to the house except the mailman and the laundry man and United Parcel. It was the wrong time of day for any of these. Perhaps it was a special-delivery letter? He went out of the workroom into the corridor and opened the front door.

13

Two men were standing outside. They wore dark suits. There was no sign of their car. 'Good morning,' said the older of the men. 'I am Mr Prentiss and this is Mr Hoxley. How are you today?'

'Fine,' Fergus said.

'We were wondering if we could perhaps come in and visit with you for a few moments?'

'What is this about?'

'Mr Hoxley thought perhaps he might explain to you some of our literature, if you would be interested.'

'We are members of the Church of the Brethren of God,' said Mr Hoxley. Both men smiled, now that this was out in the open.

'I'm afraid I'm not interested,' Fergus told them.

'Well, perhaps if we didn't come in and visit with you, you might prefer we left you some of our literature so you could acquaint yourself with it at your convenience?'

'No, really, I don't think so, thank you, I'm working, thank you. I'm very busy right now.'

'You're quite sure then, sir?' asked Mr Prentiss.

'Yes. I'm sorry. Yes, quite sure.'

'Well, then, in that case, sorry to have disturbed you, sir.'

'That's all right.'

'Good day to you then, sir,' said Mr Prentiss.

'Yes, good day to you, sir,' said Mr Hoxley.

'Good-bye,' said Fergus. He shut the door. He imagined them going off up the driveway, not speaking, humble in their dark suits and large black brogues, it being part of their visiting technique to approach each house on foot, walking all the way down that long driveway, to be rebuffed, and now walking back in the hot sun. God love them; but then, he supposed, God did. What would they have said if he had invited them in and told them that a few minutes before he had been vouchsafed a perfect vision of his dead parents? They were probably the ideal men to discuss such manifestations, and for a wild moment Fergus thought of opening the front door, calling out to them, having them turn and come back, humble Christers, labouring in the vineyard of men's souls, willing to tend *his* soul, warning him that the kingdom of heaven is at hand.

But when he went back into the workroom and looked up at

the driveway, they were gone. He switched off the electric typewriter. He saw, sitting beside the typewriter, the sheets he had arranged in a folder in case Redshields did come. But, of course, Redshields had no intention of coming. Why, he and Boweri weren't even thinking of Fergus. They were off on other deals of their own. It was up to them to get in touch with him, and they hadn't bothered. They probably had someone else working on the script right this minute. He knew it.

All right. He would go back East. He would leave here and not come back, not ever, unless it was on his terms, not theirs. But how could he? There was no money left: his wife had bled him; there was the divorce to be paid for, then his wife's bills, the divorce settlement, the alimony, the child support. Besides, if he left now, Boweri might instigate a suit against him. In the past year his life seemed to have become some other person's story, a farcical tragedy or tragical farce from which he was trying to emerge and start a new life. With Dani. But his hope for a new life had been precisely the cause of this morning's fight with her. He had wakened from a jumbled mixture of minatory dreams to see beside him on the pillow the pleasing picture of Dani's silky red hair. Aroused, he had begun to kiss and fondle her, starting their day by making love to her. After which, happy and optimistic, he had talked of taking her abroad to show her all those places she had never seen – London, Rome, Stockholm, Dublin, and, of course, Paris.

'Could we get all that into a two-week vacation?' Dani asked, interrupting him.

'My divorce will be through by then,' he said. 'You'll be able to give up your job.'

'Please!'

'Please, what?'

'You promised not to talk about that.'

'Not to talk about what?'

'Marriage,' she said. 'Us getting married. You promised not to talk about it anymore.'

'Oh, come on. Why not?'

'Because.'

'Because why?'

'Look,' she said, moving from irritation to anger. 'Just shut up about it, please?'

'Oh, come on, what is this, some superstition? The divorce will come through, don't worry about it.'

'I'm not worried, Fergus. I told you. I'm happy now.'

He had remembered Boweri. Women want to be married, Boweri had said. All women, Boweri had said.

'Look. Women want to be married,' he told her. It was as though Boweri had put the words into his mouth.

'Shit!'

'What do you mean, shit?'

'What do I mean, shit?' Dani said. 'I mean *shit!* Shit-shit-shit!'

'Now, take it easy, darling, no need to lose your temper. I was just trying to discuss the situation, that's all.'

That was when she got out of bed and, swift, naked, went into the bathroom. When she came out, he thought of Ben Jonson:

> Still to be dresst, still to be neat,
> As you were going to a feast.

Young Miss California in a miniskirt, waist-length red hair, a schoolgirl bow tied in it. She was beautiful. He knew he was too old for her. How did you talk to someone like that? He tried to smile at her. She ignored his smile.

He should have apologized: now it would be *angst* all day, for it was hopeless to phone her at her office. 'Is this a personal call?' No, it is not. 'Then what is it in connection with, please?' Oh, screw it, it wasn't his fault, you couldn't *always* say the right thing. Just one sentence wrong, not a row, just one sentence he shouldn't have said. But then, wasn't every row one sentence that shouldn't have been said? It was so easy to make mistakes with someone from another country, of another generation, someone from *California*, for godsakes.

And so Dani had left the house, angry, driving thirty miles to her work in Los Angeles without even a cup of coffee to start her day. While he had wept and had a vision. Remembering this, he went into the kitchen and put coffee in the grinder. I will start all over again as though nothing extraordinary happened, he told himself. I will have some coffee, and I will start work. Yet, as he ground the coffee, Fergus felt his tears come back. Why do I weep? he asked himself. Is it because tears ease me?

I am afraid I will lose her. That's why I weep.

'Dani? That little broad?'

Standing there in the kitchen, staring at the coffee beans hopping noisily in the grinder, Fergus remembered Boweri saying that, remembered Boweri as he had said it, sitting in his mansion in Bel-Air in the room he called his 'think tank'. Boweri, immense and smiling, shutting his ovoid eyes as he tilted his broad, almost oriental face up to catch the sunlight which came through an opened window, his smile showing white, capped teeth. As Boweri's smile became a chuckle, his breasts trembled beneath his yellow woollen playshirt and his left hand, in a familiar gesture, reached for and cradled the great soft bulge of his genitals.

'She's not so little,' Fergus told Boweri. 'As a matter of fact, she's fairly tall.'

And at once felt foolish, for in all probability Boweri was referring not to size, but to station. To Boweri a 'big' woman was someone like Elizabeth Taylor, the film star. But, as so often happened, Boweri did not seem to hear what Fergus said. Still chuckling, his eyes closed, Boweri turned away from the sunlight, shaking his head as though Fergus were a favoured, foolish son.

'Mahvelous,' Boweri said. 'Just mahvelous. Why, I think that is just great. I'm happy for you, you know. Bring her over sometime. We'll go to the races.'

But, of course, Fergus did not bring Dani over. Nor did he introduce her to Redshields. When he incautiously mentioned to Redshields that he was living with a girl, Redshields at once asked how old was she? When Fergus said twenty-two, Redshields said: 'That's nudging it. That's getting up there. Believe me,' Redshields said, 'I never screw anything over twenty if I can help it. You don't need to, anymore. These kids all lie down, they think nothing of it. You should try a piece of eighteen-year-old ass. I tell you.'

Yet Redshields is the animal who characterized my writing as 'lacking warmth' and advised me to 'tell an honest love story about normal human relationships,' Fergus thought. Is it any

wonder I'm beginning to see visions first thing in the morning?
'Bad companions.'

The voice was loud, as though its owner were trying to shout over the crackle of the coffee grinder. Fergus turned the grinder off. Father Kinneally stood, holding open the refrigerator door, looking into the refrigerator as though searching for something to eat. Fergus saw the remembered halo of baldness at the back of Father's head, around which his black hair curled inefficiently, that same hair which, on his cheekbones, sprouted irrepressible, even appearing in curious little tufts under the lenses of his thin, steel-rimmed spectacles. Bending forward as he spoke, peering into the refrigerator's recesses, Father Kinneally made a habitual motion, pressing his tongue against the inside of his lower lip so that the lip was pushed forward in an ugly monkeyface. 'Oh, Blessed Mother of Jesus,' Father Kinneally said in that special whine which indicated that he had lapsed into prayer. 'Intercede, we beseech thee, with thy Divine Son, ask Him to grant to this boy the courage to resist these evil companions, to overcome his own weakness, to turn away once and for all from that which endangers his immortal soul. Amen.'

'Gosh,' said Fergus, reverting to schoolboy diction. 'Comps Kinneally. Father Maurice Kinneally, M.A., Doctor of Divinity.'

Father Kinneally nodded as though confirming his degrees, and reaching into the refrigerator, took out a grape. He held the grape between thumb and forefinger, examining it carefully. Fergus looked at Father's large black boots, at his chin, which should be shaved twice a day and was not, and, with a shock, realized that he himself was now the age Father Kinneally had been when Father Kinneally taught him English at St Michan's College. He remembered hearing that, in his old age, Father Kinneally had been pensioned off and sent to be a parish priest in a village in Down, but it was impossible to imagine him acting as a parish priest, impossible to imagine him, say, hearing the confession of a married woman, he, who would blush scarlet if any boy's mother asked him a question on Sports Day. Yet in class and in chapel Father Kinneally had been an expert on women's wiles, a captain in the Church Militant, ever ready to defend the souls of the boys in his care against the devil and all his female hordes.

'You know, Father,' Fergus said, 'there's one thing I always wanted to ask you. Was it really true that you once went into the school dentist's office and cut all the corset and brassiere ads out of the magazines on the dentist's waiting-room table?'

Father Kinneally, still examining the grape, half-nodded in a gesture which could mean yes or no. 'Did the dentist, Mr – ah – Findlater, did *he* tell you that?'

'Yes, Conor Findlater. He married a woman who was a great friend of my mother's. He told me about it, long after I'd left school.'

Father Kinneally put the grape into his mouth, transferring it with his tongue to his right cheek, where it bulged slightly before he decided to bite on it. 'There were young boys looking at those suggestive drawings,' Father Kinneally said. 'I thought it wise. Remember, an occasion of sin is an occasion of sin, even if it is not intended to be.'

'So it *was* true.' Fergus found himself beginning to smile, but Father Kinneally's eyes, righteous behind his steelrims, fixed Fergus in warning.

'You can laugh, Fergus Fadden, oh, yes, laugh away. But I believe we were discussing something more serious. I believe we were discussing your fellow worker, Mr Redshields. We were talking about his conduct – misconduct would be more like it. Offences not only against the laws of God, but against the laws laid down by men in any decent community in this world. Would you introduce this man Redshields to your niece?'

'My *niece?*'

'Yes, your niece, your sister's girl in Dundalk, little Peggy. She's seventeen now. Would you?'

'No,' said Fergus. 'Score one for you.'

'Not that you yourself are in any position to cast the first stone,' Father Kinneally said. 'I think of that young girl who left here not an hour ago, the one beside whom you woke this morning in a state of nature, your bare flesh against her bare flesh, the young girl with whom you began your day, with no thought of the God above you or the damnation that awaits you, committing with that girl mortal sins of intent, of sight, of smell, of touch, defiling a vessel made by God, in indecent, lascivious, immoral, carnal acts too terrible to mention aloud. You, sir, I'll tell you what you are, you are a moral cesspool. If we split you open with a knife, the stench of your soul would stink in putrefaction from here to Cork!'

'What do you know about it?' Fergus said. 'You never were with a woman in your life.'

'It is not necessary to sin to know sin!'

'God help you,' Fergus said. 'Do you know what? You were a repressed fag, that's what. Now that I'm grown up, it's perfectly plain to me what you were. Imagine letting the likes of you lecture young boys about sex. Talk about a bad influence!'

'God forgive you,' Father Kinneally said. He took off his spectacles, produced a slightly soiled white handkerchief from the sleeve of his soutane, and blew his nose with some emotion.

'I always thought,' Father Kinneally said, 'that of all the boys I taught over the years, you, Fergus, had a real ability, a genuine talent for writing essays. Unfortunately, in the Senior Matriculation Examination you did not quite fulfil the extremely high hopes I had for you, but nevertheless, Fergus, I took special pains to encourage you, and, in all humility, I think I can say that if you have had any subsequent success in the literary field, I am, in some small measure, responsible. Is that not so?'

'Yes, Father. You're right. I'm sorry. But, listen, I mean, the thing is, you're just an hallucination, I've imagined you, but it *is* amazing, isn't it, how we can stand here talking as though you were really in this room? I feel as though I could reach out and touch you.'

'Don't touch me!' said Father Kinneally in a very angry voice. '*Don't touch me!*' He pushed the refrigerator door, and the door swung towards Fergus, blocking Father Kinneally from his view. Fergus caught hold of the door, and when he pushed it to shut it, Father Kinneally was not behind the door. Instead, Fergus's mother stood where the priest had been, dressed not as she had been earlier, and not as Fergus remembered her, but as the young married woman he had seen in family photograph albums. She wore a black dress and a black cloche hat. Around her neck were long knotted ropes of imitation pearls. She carried her missal in her left hand as though she had just come from church, and wore a corsage of white carnations which suggested that the church event had been a wedding or a christening. From her bulk (he had never seen her so big in life) Fergus deduced she must be pregnant. 'I am mortified,' his mother said. 'Imagine saying the like of that to a priest. I have a good mind to take down your trousers this minute and give you a good warming on your bare b.t.m.'

'Your hair was a chestnut colour,' Fergus said. 'I'd forgotten that. I wonder why I remember it now? Are you pregnant, Mama?'

'I must say your father gave me a great time that first year we were married,' his mother said. She smiled, reminiscent, looking past Fergus at the kitchen stove. 'Yes, we went out a lot, dances and parties and theatre; oh, we were out four or five nights a week. But, after that year, my troubles began. All four of you. I was always expecting. And misses. I had quite a few of those.'

'History was against you,' Fergus said. 'Imagine if you could be born, say, twenty years from now, when birth control will be permitted for Catholics?'

His mother looked back at him, and then, as she had often done when some crisis threatened, turned from him and called. 'James? James. Come in here, please?'

Fergus's father, bored, wearing his brown tweed suit, a cigarette dangling from his mouth, came into the kitchen. 'Yes, what is it, dear?'

'James, I wish you'd speak to this boy. Birth control is a mortal sin. No Catholic should discuss it, let alone say what Fergus has just said to me.'

'What's this, what's this?' Dr Fadden asked.

'Hello, Daddy,' Fergus said. His father looked at him strangely. 'We were talking about birth control,' Fergus said. 'Did you know that, nowadays, the Catholic Church is split down the middle on whether to ban it or to permit it?'

'Bunkum.'

'It's not bunkum. Things have changed.'

'Nonsense,' his father said. 'Why, that's the law of the church, and the laws of the church don't change. They haven't changed in two thousand years.'

'They're changing now, Daddy.'

'Who is this chap?' Fergus's father said, turning to Fergus's mother.

'It's Fergus, dear.'

'Who?' His father put his spectacles on his nose and stared at Fergus. 'Sedentary,' his father said, as though talking to himself. 'Bit overweight, nothing serious. Slight tremor in the hands. Neurasthenic type, not a working man. Odd clothes, though. Those damn awful shoes. Gutta-percha soles. Gutties, we used to call them.'

'But I keep telling you, dear,' Fergus's mother said. 'It's our Fergus.'

'Our Fergus? This chap? Far too old.'

'I'm thirty-nine,' Fergus said. 'You've been dead twenty-one years.'

'He's a foreigner of some sort,' his father said to his mother. 'I'd say he's a Yank.'

'Yes, he went to America,' Fergus's mother said. 'He emigrated after you died, dear.'

'America?' His father shook his head. 'Oh, I don't think so, not anyone from our family. Why, you know the old saying down in the country, they say – "It's a very low class of a person that has to cross the water to America" – did you never hear that saying, dear? It's common down in County Louth. And some truth in it, too, if the Irish-Americans one reads about are anything to go by. Prizefighters and such.'

'What about President Kennedy?' Fergus asked.

'Sorry, I didn't catch the name.'

'Kennedy. John F. Kennedy.'

'Is that your name?' said his father.

'No, James, I keep telling you. This is Fergus, our second boy.'

His father let his pince-nez drop from his nose. The small spectacles plummeted on their black silk ribbon, then spun like a yo-yo. 'Hmm,' his father said. 'What ever became of Jim?'

'Jim is practising in Belfast,' Fergus's mother said.

'Followed in my footsteps, did he?' Dr Fadden said. 'Surgery, I'll bet.'

'No. Just general practice,' Fergus said.

'But doing very well,' Fergus's mother said.

'A G.P.?' Dr Fadden said. 'Why didn't he specialize?'

'He didn't have the money, James. I was left in a very bad way when you passed on.'

'Bunkum. Not having money never stopped me. There are always scholarships. Apply yourself, and you can finance your education. I did. And in my day it was a damn sight harder than it is now, let me tell you. But I paid my own school fees. Every blessed penny of them.'

'I know,' Fergus said. 'Oh, lord, do I know!'

His father began to cough, removed the cigarette from his lips, and looked about for an ashtray. Fergus found him one. 'Speaking of Fergus,' his father said. 'Sometimes I wonder what will become of that boy.'

'In case you're interested –' Fergus began.

'Don't interrupt your father when he's speaking!' Fergus's mother warned.

'Yes, I worry about that boy,' Fergus's father said. 'It's not brains he lacks, it's application. Imagine not passing his exams! Tch, tch! In my day, I settled for nothing less than honours. Even if I got a credit – that was higher than a pass mark – I'd feel I'd done quite badly.'

'But he did very well, dear,' Fergus's mother said.

'Of course I did well,' his father said.

'Not you, dear. Fergus. He became a journalist and a writer. He's written two novels. They were quite well thought of.'

'Hmm,' said Dr Fadden. 'Remember that brooch I gave you, the one that's made out of a gold medal? I won that medal in my school days, first prize in Ireland for a school essay, senior division.'

'Yes, dear. But, as I was saying, Fergus is a professional author.'

'Hah,' said his father. 'Well, now. Makes some money out of it, does he?'

'He seems to be doing quiet well.'

'I doubt it,' his father said. 'I know a few authors. Take John O'Hare, he's what you might call a literary man. I remember John saying it's very, very difficult to make a living by one's pen. John taught school. Had to.'

'John O'Hare,' Fergus said. 'A tenth-rate trashmonger writing sentimental essays for the *Irish Mail*. Call that an author!'

'I have a couple of John's books, someplace,' Dr Fadden said. '*Old Ulster Times* is one. I don't remember the title of the other one. Both inscribed to me. He's a patient of mine.'

'But I'm a real author, Daddy. Look, I'm in *Who's Who*!'

'So are a lot of other ruffians,' said his father. 'Who writes *Who's Who*, hmm? And who cares? A lot of British snobbery-jobbery, if you ask me. There are a lot more good men out of its pages than in it. Hmm?'

'I agree with you,' Fergus said. 'But still. I thought you'd be pleased to know that I became a writer. I remember you had no great hopes that I'd amount to anything.'

His father turned from him and looked through the glass doors at the sea. Waves in slow motion tumbled, white, breaking on the sands. 'Yes,' his father said. 'Yes, I was worried.'

'But you didn't have to worry,' Fergus said. 'The *Observer* – I remember you used to swear by the *Observer*. Well, the *Observer* gave a very good review of my last book.'

'The *Observer*, eh?' his father said, turning from the glass doors, smiling at Fergus's mother. 'Did you hear that, dear?'

'Yes, dear, it's very good, isn't it?'

'First-rate,' said Dr Fadden. 'Fergus, eh? That's a surprise.'

'Daddy, I don't want to boast. No, that's not true, I do want to boast. Especially since you died thinking I was a sort of drop-out. I've written two novels. The last one was published in six countries. And before that, in New York, I wrote articles for all the American national magazines. And British magazines too. The weekly papers, you know? *New Statesman, Spectator*, and so on.'

'Well, I suppose you take that from my side of the family,' his father said. 'You were good at English, I remember that. You know, I've written one or two things myself, not that I labour under any illusions as to my status as a literary man. But I remember on the occasion of the Centenary of St Michan's College, the editors of the *Michanian*, the school magazine, asked me to write something. I wrote a memoir of Alec Hickey, one of our most brilliant alumni and a boyhood friend of mine. And when Bishop Malone retired I wrote an appreciation of him for the *Irish Mail*. And in the *Practitioner*, I wrote an article, oh, years ago, you wouldn't recall it, but it was about Catholic medicine in Ulster.'

'*I* remember it, dear,' Fergus's mother said. 'You were courting me at the time. You brought me a copy.'

'Did I? Anyway, it was well received. I remember that.'

'Yes, dear. Everybody said it was very good.'

'So, I suppose a talent for writing runs in the family,' Dr Fadden said. 'Funny, I've always thought it was, in a way, an accident of fate, my taking up medicine and not, say, the law or a teaching career. Or the priesthood! Sermons and so on. I could have used my gifts of composition. I remember saying to Canon Small – Willie Small, we were boys at school together – I said, "Willie," I said, "if I'd taken Holy Orders, I bet you I'd be a monsignor today." "No, James," he said – he was an awfully nice chap, Willie, God rest his soul – "No, James," he said. " *You* would be a bishop!" ' Fergus's father smiled and shook his head, remembering. 'A bishop,' he repeated. 'Most Reverend Dr Fadden, Bishop of Down and Connor. Hmm.'

'I know, dear,' Fergus's mother said gently. 'But Fergus is trying to tell you what *he's* done. You have to encourage them, you know. Let them see that you take an interest.' She turned to Fergus, crinkling up her eyes in a wise, 'grown-up' smile. 'Your last book is awfully good, Fergie. Show it to your father. I'm sure he'll be pleased.'

'No, forget it,' Fergus said.

'Go on. Get a copy and show it to him. He'll be interested, really he will.'

'I don't know where they are,' Fergus lied.

'Your father is interested in every one of you,' his mother said. 'We don't have favourites.'

'No?' Fergus said. A hot, tight feeling rose in his chest. He turned away, walked past his father and mother, and went into the living room. He sat on the orange armchair, staring mistily at the sneakers which his father called 'gutties'.

'He's very high strung,' he heard his mother whisper.

'No two children are the same,' his father said. 'Funny, he's just the opposite of Jim.'

'He takes things very hard, poor wee man.'

'I know,' his father said. 'I'll have a word with him. Poor old chap.'

'Yes, James, I wish you would.'

He could not bear to have his father speak to him as a grown-up, placating a child. He jumped up from the orange armchair, went to the glass doors, and tried to open them. But he had locked them earlier. He leaned his forehead against the cool glass, and as he did, sensed that his father had come up and was standing directly behind him. 'You know very well,' his father said, 'that if I were around I'd be proud about your writing, I'd be pleased as punch. Hmm?'

It was true, he supposed. He stared, through the glass, at the sea.

'Yes, I'd be delighted about your writing,' his father continued. 'But, your present life, well, that's another matter. Thank God I'm not around to make judgements on *that*. I should hope, though, that if I were, I'd be kinder to you than you are to me.'

Which could be true. Penitent, Fergus turned from his inspection of the sea, ready to make some apology. But the room, behind him, was empty. He looked towards the kitchen, which was also empty. On the sideboard, the electric kettle hissed in a way which warned that almost all the water had evaporated. He went into the kitchen and pulled out the kettle's plug. If my father *could* come back, he thought, it would have happened like this. But dammit, he *did* come back, I saw him, he was right there. You had better go and sit down, he told himself. Never mind coffee. This has got to stop. Whatever it is that's getting you into this state, it's got to stop.

He turned and went into the living room and sat on the yellow sofa. His heart beat alarmingly. Tachycardia, the doctor had said, it's your nerves. 'Look,' Dani had told him. 'For days, you've been saying you're going to phone Redshields and clear this thing up. Yet every evening, when I come home, you've done nothing about it, you've simply sat around all day letting it get to you. Phone him! Nothing's worse than not knowing.'

'You're wrong. I don't give a damn.'

'You do give a damn, Fergus. You need the bread. That's why you came out here in the first place, right? Because of the divorce.'

'Right.'

'So stop pretending you don't care. Pick up the phone and call him. Better you get mad at him than at me.'

Which was true. But it was humiliating. Dammit, he hated being anyone's employee, ever! Perhaps if he phoned Redshields now, not mentioning the script, but in a joking way said to Redshields, do you know what, I had this extraordinary extrasensory experience this morning, I wanted to tell you about it, I mean I could have sworn I was standing here talking to my dead father. You're interested in that sort of thing, Norman – tell me, did anything like that ever happen to you? A social telephone call. No mention of work. He could imagine Redshields listening, or pretending to listen, for, even on the telephone, Redshields acted out his 'listening' tricks, removing his thick-lensed spectacles the better to show that his eyes were thoughtful, nodding from time to time, saying 'Fantaastic!' and 'Interesting!', for Redshields believed that if you showed interest in this way you could convince anyone, even a stupid actor, that he or she was a person you were 'relating' to, and, as Redshields himself put it, 'When you relate to a person you are making contact with that person as a human being, which is the name of the game, which is where it's at. Right?'

Perhaps, though, Fergus reflected, the fact that Redshields invariably uses the clichés of the moment *does* indicate that he listens to what's said to him. For when Redshields adopts a word or phrase, it's invariably at the precise point in time when that word or phrase has become a cliché. Similarly, when Redshields drops it, it is an infallible sign that the cliché has disappeared from current usage. This held true, Fergus decided, not only for words but for styles in books, music, clothing, interior decoration, and political thought. He remembered his first meeting with Redshields (ostensibly a social occasion, dinner at Redshields's house, but with the understanding that they would spend some time discussing the film which Fergus had been hired to write and Redshields to direct). He had been met at the front door by Redshields, who proved to be a short, stout man in his middle forties, bespectacled, naked except for a pair of chino pants, his hairless body silvered with sweat, his little Buddha belly bulging from the waistband of his trousers, long, fair, womanish hair curling in ringlets about his neck and ears, a man who was a film director by avocation but, in reality, like many of his kind, a salesman, a carnival barker who, from the moment he opened the door to Fergus, gave no conversational quarter: 'Well, come in, so here you are, you found the place, how are you, hey, good to see you, let's go in here, yeah, right in here into my private little shithole, buried in this goddam big palazzo, my own room, yes, Daddy, I got my own room at last, well, how are you, are you enjoying Los Angeles, no, don't answer that, let me say this, first, I myself hate this town with a passion, I despise it, it makes me sick to my stomach, I mean physically, upchuck, sick, if it wasn't for my family and a few good friends and my music and my books, look, by the way I want you to hear something, sit here, in this chair, you have speakers coming at you from that corner and that corner and up there in the ceiling, perfect acoustics, no kidding! Now! I want your opinion, this record I just got sent me from London, this guy is fantaastic, see what you think, he's the Nigerian Liszt, no kidding. Now, sit, listen, enjoy.'

Bach, ear-filling, had come simultaneous and sudden from every side, pitched as no music ever heard by the ear of Bach, a dum-dum bullet of sound, spreading, deadening. Redshields, standing by the console, pantomimed delight, then, motioning Fergus to sit back and relax, abruptly left the room. Fergus sat looking at the marble-topped desk, piled with letters, bills, brochures for camera gear; at a strange assortment of novels and scripts littered on a long trestle table; at the framed colour photographs of Redshields's small daughter, smiling through steel teeth braces; at an unidentifiable, amateurish abstract painting; at a wall hung with framed photographs of Redshields shaking hands with a former American President, Redshields arm-in-arm with film stars, Redshields being presented with a film award by the Premier of Yugoslavia. The fugue ended and a prelude began. Suddenly, through a large picture window, Fergus saw Redshields appear in the garden outside, moving among various trees, plucking fruit from their branches, putting the fruit into a wooden bowl. Redshields disappeared, and then, a moment later, his footsteps muted by the giant crash of piano hammers, bounded back into the room where Fergus sat, bearing the wooden bowl which contained a grapefruit, lemons, limes, kumquats, an orange; prancing to the window to point out the trees; indicating that these fruits did indeed come from those very trees in that very garden and now must be eaten and enjoyed for their delicious freshness. Inexorably the preludes and fugues continued throughout this dumbshow, which ended when Redshields pretended to sit and listen, then, suddenly, miming that an electric light bulb had gone off inside his skull, bounded up, picked up the telephone jack, thirty-foot extension and all, showing that he must make a phone call, and scooted out of the room, shutting the door behind him, leaving Fergus for a further fifteen minutes in solitary confinement with the deafening piano of the Nigerian Liszt.

We never did talk about the film that evening, Fergus remembered. Perhaps Redshields didn't want to talk about it. Certainly the moment never presented itself, for when Redshields's attention was not wholly claimed by the temper tantrums of his five-year-old daughter, who ate with them, or a screaming argument with his wife on the demerits of Los Angeles as a place to live, phone calls incoming and outgoing made sustained conversation impossible. Which was normal. Direct conversation was, to Redshields, a secondary form of communication. When he moved from the orbit of his house to an office, restaurant, airport, a new city, a new country, his telephone-answering service tracked his progress, keeping him always in touch. On arrival at any new place, Redshields's post-greeting words were invariably: 'Any calls?' followed by a request to use the phone and check with his service. Calls, local, long distance, intercity, intercontinental, endless talkings to New York and London, telephone receiver jammed between ear and hunched shoulder, greeting, cajoling, advising, shouting, laughing, kibitzing, earnest, abrupt, decisive, angry, hurt, outraged, resigned, a non-stop performance, an endless spin-off of names, stars, agents, 'properties', financing arrangements, turning and turning in the widening gyre of Redshields's schemes, for almost all of his calls produced no tangible results, they were lottery tickets, part of a gamble which once in a hundred ploys might show some return. The telephone was, quite simply, more real to Redshields than anything that happened outside its circuits. On it and in it and through it, he lived his life.

And yet . . . and yet, Fergus thought, with all that phoning, with all that cradling of receivers and shouts of 'Hi, what's new?

Listen, glad you called!' Redshields has not phoned me in three weeks. He may never call again unless I make the first move. Dani's right. I've got to stop sitting here, day after day, waiting. Look what's happening. I'm starting to hold conversations with the dead. I'm like a ghost myself. I've got to do something to break this spell. All right, I will, this time I will. None of this business of them telling me he'll call me back. I'll insist that he talk to me. Now.

Fergus picked up the phone. He didn't have to look up the number. He knew it. He didn't have to dial. Or speak. In fact, he knew just exactly what would happen. It would go like this.

'Redbo Productions, good morning,' a female voice would say.

'May I speak to Mr Redshields, please?'

'Mr Redshields's office, good morning,' a second female voice would say.

'This is Mr Fadden. Is Norman there?'

'Oh, hi, Mr Fadden, I'm sorry, but Mr Redshields is in conference right now. I can't interrupt him.'

'I want to talk to him, it's urgent.'

'Are you at home, Mr Fadden?'

'Yes.'

'Well, I have your number, we'll call you right back, okay?'

'No, not okay, this is an emergency, I have to talk to him now. Please?'

'Well, just a moment, Mr Fadden –' and a pause while she'd secretly get in touch with Redshields and be told by Redshields to say he was busy and get rid of this guy! And then she'd come back on: 'Mr Fadden? I'm real sorry, but I just can't seem to reach Mr Redshields right this minute, he's turned his phone off.'

'Well, go in and tell him. I told you, it's urgent! Please?'

Then another pause, and then she'd say: 'I'll see what I can do –' and another pause and then, click!

Redshields: 'Hey, Fergus, how are you, good to hear from you, listen, Ferg, listen, can I get back to you, there's something very exciting I want to talk to you about, but I'm in a meeting right now [tiny whisper] – *can't talk* . . . Okay? Get back to you, okay?'

But Fergus would be firm, he would be absolutely firm and say,

'Norman, I told your secretary, this is urgent. If you can't talk in there, go in the other room.'

The line would go quiet. (While Redshields thought.) And then: 'Okay, hold it a minute –' and a moment later Redshields would pick up the receiver in his outer office, his voice decisive and irritated. 'Okay, so what is it? World War Three?'

And then, Fergus thought, what can I say, what *will* I say? I will have him on the phone at last, all right, so I'll say, let's see, I'll say – ah! –

'Norman, I just wanted to tell you that I'm leaving this afternoon. Leaving California. As a matter of fact, I'm going to Paris for a month.' I mean, that will let him know I'm through, he's not getting any more revisions from me, that I realize they've probably hired somebody else to rewrite what I wrote for them, they're not fooling me, they never did. What will he say then?

'Paris, eh? Well, that's terrific! I hate you! Why do you writers have all the fun?'

I mean, what if he says that? What if he never even mentions the work? What if he then says: 'So what's the crisis, man?'

(What do *I* say?)

'Well, I just thought I'd better tell you I'm leaving. I mean right now. And also I want to tell you I think you've treated me disgracefully –' (No, I can't say that, it sounds childish.) I have to make the point, somehow, that I wrote this film script in good faith, I made some of the changes they asked for, and I delivered the completed work to them three weeks ago, and, under the contract, if I haven't heard from them in two weeks, I am to assume that my services are no longer required, at least that's what my agent tells me, so, therefore, all I want is for them to pay me the rest of the money they promised and dismiss me, and no hard feelings, believe me, I don't care what they do at this point, I'm sick of Redshields going on about the art of film, he wouldn't know art if it came up and sat on his face – I'll phone him up right now and tell him that. 'Do you hear me, Norman, you wouldn't know what art was if it came up and sat on your face!' But what would be the use of saying that, he wouldn't even get angry, he'd sound surprised, he'd say something like: 'Well, Fergus, I'm honestly very, very disappointed to hear that you feel that way, because I have the greatest respect for you as a creative person, and I thought we had a very good experience working together, et cetera –' and then he'd put down the phone and call Boweri, who would stop payment on what they owe me and start a suit against me for breach of contract, and the next thing, I'd be in the hands of their lawyers, and the whole purpose of coming out here to write this film and pay off my divorce would be up in smoke, and I'd be worse off than before. God, how do other writers deal with these situations? How did, say, Faulkner manage to come out here time after time and take the money and run, when I can't even handle one job?

The thought of Faulkner steadied Fergus, for Faulkner had endured and prevailed over this stoop labour in the Hollywood vineyard. If Faulkner started seeing his dead parents first thing in the morning, he would settle right in and make use of it.

'James, where are you?'

His mother's voice, in the corridor. Fergus turned to look, and as he did, his mother came into the living room, still wearing her black cloche hat but now carrying two prayerbooks and an umbrella. She stopped, apologetically, at sight of Fergus. 'Oh, excuse me. Are you making a telephone call?'

'No,' said Fergus. He looked at the receiver in his hand and replaced it on its cradle.

'James?' his mother called again. 'Where *is* your father?' she said to Fergus. 'We'll have to hurry if we're to catch the eleven-o'clock mass.'

'It's not Sunday.'

'Of course it's not Sunday. But it's a Holiday of Obligation!' his mother said, scandalized. 'Oh, where *is* your father?'

'Please,' Fergus said. 'Don't go. I want to talk to you. There are so many things I want to ask both of you. Important things.'

His father came into the living room, drawing on a pair of yellow chamois gloves. 'Nothing's more important than a person's religious duties,' his father said. 'Are you ready, dear?'

'Ready? I've been waiting for ages,' his mother said. She handed his father a prayerbook, an old brown missal Fergus remembered well, bulged to twice its original size with mass cards commemorating dead friends and relatives.

'But the nearest church is miles away,' Fergus said. 'Please, Daddy. Stay and talk to me.'

'Come along, dear,' Dr Fadden said, ignoring Fergus, taking his wife's arm, walking her briskly down the corridor.

'If you're going to mass,' Fergus called, 'then, does that mean, there *is* an afterlife? Heaven and hell?'

'Mustn't miss the first gospel,' Dr Fadden said. He opened the front door. 'Rain?' he asked, stretching out his hand, palm upward, in a remembered gesture.

'No, no, it's a lovely day, James,' Fergus's mother said. Both parents stepped out onto the front porch; then his father shut the front door, leaving Fergus alone in the corridor. Fergus went to the door and opened it. He went out. There was no one outside. Dry leaves, shed by the eucalyptus tree in the driveway, rustled, dragging across the concrete walk. 'Daddy?' Fergus called. 'Mama?' The sun blinded him. He put his hand up, shading his eyes, and at that moment, to his left, saw two men on the roof of the house next door. They were television repairmen with walkie-talkies in their hands. They were looking down at him. He imagined them in a courtroom, dressed in their green coveralls, giving testimony. 'Yes, we were at Mr Killan's, adjusting the aerial for Channel Ten reception, when this guy came out the front door. Yes, the house next door. We could see him standing in his driveway.'

'Was he intoxicated?'

'Well, I don't know, but he called out "Daddy?" and then he called out "Mama." That right, Burt?'

'Thass right.'

'And there was no one else in the driveway?'

'No, sir. Not a soul.'

The television repairmen were moving around on Killan's roof. Fergus heard a squawk on the walkie-talkie. 'Go to the left a piece. Over.'

'Hi.' Fergus waved to the men. He tried a smile.

'Hi, there,' one of the men said. Fergus turned and went back inside.

*

He shut the door. In his childhood, playing hide-and-seek, there would come a moment when he'd want the game to end: if only the others would give up; no more scary shrieks and jumping out of dark corners. Now, in the brick-tiled corridor he caught his breath in alarm as, behind him, something hit like a sandbag against the window. He turned and saw a bird, wings beating as it butted its head, its beak, its claws, against the glass barrier it could not see. He raised his hands and went towards the corridor window, shooing the bird off; saw it stall, hover, then swoop up and over the roof. Behind the house were mountain slopes, with clumps of chaparral and, here and there, tall century plants like viziers' staffs, blooming once a year with strange feathery foliage, a landscape existing contiguously in his mind as a real range of mountains and also as a fantasy backdrop from which, rearing out of the film screens of his childhood, Hollywood cowboys might clatter through a mountain gulch. The house, like this landscape, existed both in the present and in his past, as this real house by the sea in California and as the house he now imagined it was, that house overlooking Belfast Lough, with a view of distant shipyard gantries, the house he was born in. Somewhere, in these rooms, hidden in closets, under beds, those others waited, filled with malicious, anticipatory glee, waited to jump out, yell, make his heart thump. If only he could, if only they would, let him stop, let him call '*Pax!*'

He stood now in the corridor, his back to the living room, hardly able to believe that a few moments ago, far from fleeing his ghosts, he had pursued them with questions. And, even harder to believe, he had sat in the living room unable to phone Redshields; for Redshields, the film, Boweri, his divorce – all the worries of a normal day seemed as nothing to these new fears. Until now, he had thought that, like everyone else, he exorcised his past by living it. But he was not like everyone else, His past had risen up this morning, vivid, uncontrollable, shouldering into his present. How can I live a life with Dani, he wondered, if my mother keeps coming into the room?

He turned and looked back into the living room. There, and in the kitchen, and on the terrace outside: that was where he had seen them. He would not go back into that part of the house; he would go the other way, into the back bedroom, with its two sets of bunk beds, where, during summer rentals, people stacked their children to sleep. He would go in there and sit down calmly and think himself back into a normal frame of mind. He went down the hall and opened the bedroom door. It was a cold room with a stone floor; there were cardboard boxes overflowing with abandoned clothes. On the dresser were ladies' lamps without lampshades; a sleeping bag was slung over one of the two rocking chairs; near the door was a pile of ladies' fashion magazines tied with twine, and on top of the pile, pitched forward as though it had stumbled, was a large, bedraggled Mexican piñata donkey made of red and blue paper. He went in and stood, his hand on the door handle, looking around in the silence of storeroom junk.

'Close the door, dear, there's a draught.'

Aunt Mary was in the lower bunk.

His heart caught. He started to back out of the room, but she laughed and beckoned. 'Come on in,' she said. 'I declare to God, you'd think you were afraid of me.'

Afraid of her, he shut the door and stood facing her.

'That's the boy,' she said. Although she was in bed and under the blankets, she seemed fully clothed, wearing a black dress fastened at the neck by a row of small octagonal jet buttons, the sort of dress she wore in the years she lived with Fergus's parents. He remembered those little buttons: he used to pull them when she took him on her knee to read him a story. It was like her, that although she worried that he might break the buttons off, she did not stop him playing with them.

Now she pointed to the rocking chair, willing him to sit down. Sunlight, through the bedroom shutters, made prison-bar shadows on her face. 'Mary was our beauty,' his father used to say, and in a photograph Fergus had seen when Aunt Mary was bridesmaid at Aunt Rose's wedding, she was just that: a dark-haired young woman with delicate features, a long, swan neck, large, limpid eyes. There were no pictures of Aunt Mary's own wedding. Now that he had her back, he ought to ask about that.

'I know what you want,' she said.

'What?' he said.

'A yellow jujube,' she said.

He laughed. He no longer felt afraid. 'Come and sit by me,' she said. 'Do you want a story?'

'Yes.'

'What about *Grimms' Fairy Tales*?' she said. 'They're good value. You like them, don't you?'

He went to the rocking chair, and removing a broken hand hair-drier from the seat, sat down facing her. She had already picked up *Grimms' Fairy Tales* and was going through it, looking for a story to read aloud.

'Aunt Mary,' he began, 'you were always called Mrs Christie. I remember asking Mama why, but she said it was very sad, we weren't to talk about it. You had been married, she said, but your husband was dead.'

'I have red ones and green ones,' said Aunt Mary, her fingers separating sweets in a crumpled paper bag. 'And black, but you don't like black, it's Kathleen who likes the black ones. Yellow?' She shook the bag out on the book's cover. Jujubes spilled over the bedspread. 'Not a one left.'

'But your husband wasn't dead. That's what I heard later. He wasn't dead at all.'

'Tch, tch, tch,' Aunt Mary said, picking up the jujubes, putting them back in the crinkled paper bag, which she always carried in her big black purse. 'It's a good job Lent is coming. We're all eating far too many sweets, spoiling our appetites for our dinner.'

'The story I heard,' Fergus said, 'was that Daddy's mother, old Grandmother Fadden, married you off to this Christie, who was a Scottish shipbroker who came over to Killiney on a holiday and acted as though he were a millionaire. Anyway, he swept you off your feet.'

'Swept me off my feet?' Aunt Mary laughed, a false laugh, coquettish, to cover her embarrassment.

'Anyway, he married you, and Daddy went over to Scotland to give you away at the wedding in Glasgow. It was a very grand wedding, and apparently Christie *was* well off. But the other thing about him was what his family didn't tell you. Any of you. Which was that he was insane.'

Aunt Mary shrugged. 'Fergus Fadden!' said she, mock-stern. 'Where did you get hold of a yarn like that?'

'It's true,' Fergus said. 'You went on your honeymoon to Europe, and in Paris, the first night of your visit, you and he were alone in a box at the Paris Opéra when he got the idea that some man in another box was making eyes at you. So he took you home the very next day, straight back to Glasgow, and as soon as he got you there he locked you up in a room in his house, and you were a week locked up before you managed to smuggle a letter out with one of the maids, telling my father to come and get you.'

'Your poor mother, may she rest in peace, always said one thing about you, Fergus. She said, "If you tell that Fergus a story and then you hear him tell it back to someone else, well, I assure you," said she, "it will not lose in the telling." '

'So none of this is true, then, about the mad husband?' Fergus said. 'On your word of honour, it's all some lie my mother told me?'

'I didn't say that,' Aunt Mary said. 'Now, that's enough old guff, Mister Smart. Do you want me to read you a story, or don't you?'

'No, I'm telling *you* the story,' Fergus said. 'When your letter reached Ireland, my father and Davy McAusley went over to Glasgow and demanded to see you. And the upshot of it was, they took you home. You never saw Christie again. He died in an asylum, years later. But, because you left him, his family never gave you one penny. And so you lived with us all those years, working for us as a sort of unpaid maid and nurse.'

'Oh, go on with you, I was nothing of the sort,' Aunt Mary said. 'I was well looked after, I had a roof over my head and food in my mouth and all you children to keep me company; there's many a person is far worse off in this world than I was. I had my health, just a touch of bronchitis sometimes in the cold weather, but, by and large, I kept on my feet. We had some grand times, I had the best of friends, Jeanie McPartland and Davy McAusley, that you mentioned earlier. I hadn't my own house, that's true, and I'm sure sometimes your father and mother might have preferred to be alone, though, God knows, I tried not to be a nuisance. You remember very well, I spent a lot of time up in my room. I had, oh, it came to about twelve shillings a week from a stock my mother left me, and I saved up on that to buy little Christmas presents and so on. I saved up and bought my wireless set, you remember the one with the earphones, oh, the pleasure I had out of that wee box.' Aunt Mary's eyes blinked. She sniffled, took her handkerchief from her big black purse, and touched it to her nose.

'You're crying,' Fergus said.

'Crying? Did you ever hear the like? What would I be crying about, amn't I telling you about my wireless set, it was such a joy to me over the years, never had one bit of trouble with it; anyway, I'm saying I tried to be useful, your mother told me – do you remember I used to bake johnnycakes and tarts and cream puffs on Sundays? – well, your mother used to say that when I would go off to Dublin to spend a few weeks with Aunt Rose, your mother said you children always plagued her, saying, "When's Aunt Mary coming back so's we can have cream puffs and tarts and johnnycakes with jam?" ' Aunt Mary laughed. 'I was very lucky,' she said. 'I had a way with cakes and puff pastry. Your mother, now, she was grand with a roast, but she wasn't a great baker. Not that I'm comparing myself with her. I only wish I'd been half the cook Julia was.'

'But you were still a young woman when you came back from Scotland,' Fergus said. 'Didn't you ever think of getting married again?'

'I was married,' Aunt Mary said. 'To him.'

'But he was mad, he died in an asylum. You could have got an annulment.'

'Tch, tch,' Aunt Mary said. 'Illness is no cause for an annulment. In sickness and in health, you are still married to that person. You could maybe get a separation, but that wouldn't mean you could marry someone else. What sort of Catholic are you, if you don't know that?'

'But, what a waste!'

'Waste, what's a waste about it?' Aunt Mary said. 'I had my life, I had my health, I helped with you children, oh, you were the funny wee articles, the four of you. God is good, Fergus. Yes, God is good. What I pray for is to see us all together again, someday, the whole Fadden family, the way we once were, but with even more of us, my own father and mother, my sisters and brothers, my friends and relations, and you children, my little nieces and nephews, all of us reunited in heaven in the sight of Almighty God. Yes, and God willing, we will be.'

'And Christie?' Fergus asked. 'The lunatic who locked you up, but who's still your husband in the sight of the Catholic Church? Do you see him up there, in heaven, reunited with you, sitting by your side?'

'Do you mean Jack?' Aunt Mary said. 'Poor Jack. I pray for him every night. I always remember him in my prayers.'

There was a moment of silence. Aunt Mary opened her handbag, producing a small package of Sen Sens, and put a pellet on her tongue to sweeten her breath. She shut her purse with a snap. It was very quiet in the room. Fergus looked at his aunt, who, her head tilted to one side, had begun to tidy some loose strands of hair which had fallen down about her neck. Above, and sudden, a clatter filled the sky. Aunt Mary looked at him. 'An aeroplane?' He nodded. A United States Navy helicopter, down from Point Mugu on the morning run, cawed like a monster crow as it passed in shadow over the roof of the house, the wind from its rotor blades disturbing the top branches of the eucalyptus tree in the driveway. The corncrake sound diminished. Aunt Mary picked up the book of fairy tales. 'Your mother told me you're married?' she said, not looking at him, looking at the book.

'I was.'

'You have a wee girl of your own?'

'Yes.'

'What do you call her?'

'Lise.'

'Is that a saint's name?'

'It's a form of Elizabeth.'

'How old is she?'

'Ten.'

'The mother has her, then?'

'Yes.'

'Do you get to see her much? Does she come out here to visit you?'

'No.'

'I hear that's often the way of it,' Aunt Mary said.

'Well, I'm not very popular with her mother. I left, you see.'

'Well, that would annoy a person, I can see that,' Aunt Mary said. 'Yes, in my case, Jack's family, the Christies, *they* thought I should have stayed with him.'

'Sometimes,' Fergus said, 'that's just not possible.'

'Lise,' Aunt Mary said. 'That reminds me. Princess Elizabeth, did she become Queen?'

'She did.'

'And the other wee one. Princess Margaret Rose. What became of her?'

'She married a photographer.'

'Go on!' said Aunt Mary. 'Isn't it awful the time we waste talking about those ones. When I think back on my life, the time I spent reading about them, all that trashy stuff. And I had the hard time of it, finishing up any good books.'

'You always used to say that,' Fergus said. 'I mean, about not reading enough good books.'

'Well, I still say it,' Aunt Mary said.

'But wait!' Suddenly Fergus sat forward, the rocking chair going down onto its points, almost spilling him into Aunt Mary's lap. 'You say you still say it. But from where? Where are you? I mean, *is* there some other life? That's what I was asking Daddy earlier. Aunt Mary, do you know how important it would be if you could just answer me? It might be the most important discovery in – well – in history.'

'Empirical proof,' said a man's voice, muffled, a Western American voice. Someone rapped on the bedroom window. Fergus, startled, got up from the rocking chair, and there was a man outside the window, a workman in green coveralls, wearing a baseball cap with the words 'Kwik-Cable' stencilled on its peak. The man smiled agreeably as Fergus turned the swivel screw which opened the window. *Empirical proof*, Fergus said to himself, well, yes, that's what I mean. If Aunt Mary has experienced another life and has returned to tell me about it, that would be a sort of empirical proof.

'Pardon me,' said the man outside the window. 'Can I go on your roof?'

'What?'

'We're putting up a new aerial next door,' the man said. 'It's a tough one, getting the support wire up. If I could pass over your roof it would make it a whole lot easier.'

'I thought you said "proof,"' Fergus said stupidly.

'No, the roof. I'll use this ladder, is that okay, sir?'

'Of course.'

'Thanks, sir. I appreciate it,' said the workman, backing away, grinning, positioning his ladder outside the window, beginning to climb up it, moving up until only his legs were visible, then going on, out of sight. Fergus heard his footsteps as he moved across the roof. He looked back at the bunk bed and saw that Aunt Mary had slipped down to a supine position. There was a new sound in the room, and now he knew why he had been so afraid when he first saw her. For this was the sound he had heard when she lay in coma on a bed in the day nursery and he, like all the others, had to take his turn sitting by her. He was twelve then. Now, as then, her mouth was open; her false teeth had been removed. Her grey hair had come loose about her neck, spreading in heavy damp coils across the pillow, and as she slept, her breathing made a tearing noise as though someone in the room were ripping coarse sheets into shreds. He stood by the bed and looked down, frightened, as he had been long ago, and as he had done then, reached out and tugged her shoulder, trying to shake her into consciousness. But the dying woman resisted his touch. As though in a waking nightmare, everything happened again as it had happened in his boyhood. Her noisy breathing stopped, momentarily, with one abrupt, gasping intake of breath. Silence; she opened her eyes, her toothless mouth gaping wide, the eyes not seeing him at first, then focusing slowly as, in a moment of clarity, she seemed to recall who he was and where she was, and, afraid of frightening the child, reached for and picked up a novel which lay on the bedspread. She held it up, nodding to him, still gasping, trying to pretend she was all right, she was going to read, she had dozed off, and now would read, and so held the book ostentatiously in both hands, staring at its printed pages. He looked at the dust jacket of the novel, as he had looked at it long ago. The jacket was in three colours – orange, white, and green.

The title, upside down to his eye, was: *Ireland: The Orange and the Green*.

Aunt Mary was not reading the novel. She was holding the book upside down. Breathing in harsh, desperate gasps, she sat up suddenly in the bed, her hair falling about her brows, her face a sweating chalk mask in which, flickering above bluish sacs of skin, her eyes pretended, for his sake, to scan the printed page. And, as long ago, a stealthy but uncontrollable panic rose up in him. Afraid of her, he slipped off his seat and backed towards the door, finding the door handle, opening and closing the door quietly, on that harsh, terrible breathing. Escaping, wanting to run, discovering what he had first learned that day when he was a boy of twelve. Death was not something in a book. She was dying. He would die.

In the corridor he stopped and stood, his heartbeat fast, hearing loud birdsong from the bottle-brush tree outside the window. The hidden bird sounded anxious, as though warning intruders not to penetrate its territory. The bird can sing to ward off its foes, Fergus thought, but I, what can I do?

He went down the corridor and entered the workroom. He went to the big dictionary on the reading table and looked up: '*hallucination – an apparent sensory experience of something that does not exist outside the mind.*' As so often, the dictionary was no help. He sat in the large wing chair by the typewriter. In a briefcase under his desk was the novel he was writing, the book he had been forced to put aside when he came out to California. Every morning in the past three weeks of waiting for Boweri and Redshields to decide on the film script, he had briefly considered starting the novel again. Now he briefly considered it. As soon as this business was settled, he would get back to work on it. As soon as this business was settled.

The telephone rang in the living room. *As soon as this business?* But it would not be them, it would be Dani. He jumped up and ran down the corridor, glad she had called: he would apologize, he would tell her about the visions, he would –

'Mr Fadden?' A woman's voice.

'Yes.'

'This is Mr Bernard Boweri's office, Mr Fadden.'

'Oh, yes?'

'Mr Boweri wishes to know if you would be available for a meeting this afternoon?'

'At his office?' Fergus asked, for of course he would be available, he could drive in –

'No. The reason I'm calling you is Mr Boweri had another appointment at the beach. He's already left for your area. He will check with me later, and if it's convenient for you, he would like to drop by and visit with you?'

'Well, yes, of course. I live pretty far out, now, you know?'

'Yes. We have your address. Mr Boweri has checked on your location. He asked me to tell you he'll drop by between two and three, if that's okay with you?'

'Fine,' Fergus said. 'Do you know if Mr Redshields will be coming too?'

There was a pause. 'No-o, I don't believe so, I believe Mr Redshields is out of town.'

'Oh, is he?'

'Yes, I believe so. And, Mr Fadden?'

'Yes.'

'Mr Boweri said I should tell you it will be a general discussion. No specifics. Tell Mr Fadden it's just a chat, he said.'

'Oh, fine.'

'Then between two and three, okay?'

'Yes. Thank you.'

'Just a chat,' Fergus said aloud when he hung up the phone. 'No specifics. Just a general discussion,' he said aloud, mimicking the secretarial voice. 'All right, Boweri,' he said, 'let's get it out in the open, let's put our cards on the table. You don't like what I did? Right! You've hired someone else? Fine! But let's get the bloody thing over with! Dammit, I have other work to do!'

'My gracious.' An amused voice mocked him. He turned. His sister Maeve came in from the terrace, through the opened glass doors. She wore her navy tunic, black stockings, and white blouse, the school uniform of the Cross and Passion Convent. She was sixteen, in her final school year. 'Talking away to himself like some old one in a cottage behind the bogs!' Maeve said. 'Gosh, they'll be coming for you in a blue van to cart you off to the looney bin if you go on talking to people who aren't here!'

'I wasn't!' he protested, as irritated by her superior grown-up airs as he used to be when he was the younger one at home.

'You were so. Don't tell fibs. I heard you. You were talking to someone called Bow-er-i.'

'I wasn't. I was just – rehearsing – what I'm going to say to him this afternoon. Anyway, what would you know about it?'

'Look what's talking,' Maeve said. 'Who are you to talk?'

'I am someone who has had experiences you couldn't possibly understand. So, let's drop all this!'

'Experiences!' Maeve said, turning, looking at the room. 'Well, I must say I agree with you. Living here in this super place on the sea. Aren't you dead lucky! Money for jam, that's what you're getting. I wish I'd been a writer.'

'People like you have no idea how hard writers work.'

'Oh, come on! Sure these Yanks must be paying you a fortune. Writing a film! Oh, aren't you home free!'

'There are more important things than money.'

'Like what, for instance?'

'Well, like literary values.'

'Of course,' Maeve said. 'There's Shakespeare. And at the other end of the ladder there's you, F. Fadden.'

'Can't you pick anybody but Shakespeare?'

Maeve giggled. 'Who do you want? Your old hero Mr James Joyce? Wouldn't it sicken you, the Dublin people making a shrine out of that blinking Martello Tower he used to live in? Of course, it's just a trick for the Yankee tourists. The Dublin people will do anything for the almighty dollar.'

'If it was a shrine to some saint or the founder of the Total Abstinence Society, it would be all right, wouldn't it?'

'It would be an improvement. James Joyce. That cod!'

'The government has fixed up the tower Yeats lived in,' Fergus said. 'At Thoor Balee. I suppose you think that's daft, too?'

'Do you mean W. B. Yeats?'

'Yes, I mean W. B. Yeats, who the hell do you think I mean?'

'Him,' Maeve said. 'We used to have him in school, the "Lake Isle of Innisfree" – bzzzz-bzzzz-bzzzz – Sister Innocenta reciting it as though it was Holy Writ. I don't know. Did *you* like him?'

'He's considered the greatest English-speaking poet of this century.'

'*Is* he?' Maeve pulled on her lower lip, impressed. 'Of course, he's not really Irish. I mean, he was a Protestant, he's Anglo-Irish, et cetera. Still, he was in the Irish Senate, wasn't he? Och, I suppose we *could* claim him.'

'So,' said Fergus angrily. 'Miss Maeve Fadden will permit Mr W. B. Yeats to enter the Irish Pantheon.'

'But not you,' Maeve said. 'I have to leave you outside there with your hat in your hand.'

'Time will tell.'

'Oh, rocks!' Maeve said. 'Listen, talking about time, would you ever ask a person if they had a mouth on them?'

'What do you mean?'

'I mean it must be lunchtime.' In her school uniform she reminded him of some sort of tour guide. Her hair was done up in a thick braid, and on her right breast was the school badge, showing a heart, a cross, and a wreath of thorns. 'Is this the kitchen?' she said, pointing.

'Looks like it, doesn't it?'

'I'm just being polite, Fergus. I'm waiting to be asked in.'

'This way, then.'

As his shadow fell on the living-room window, the unseen bird outside set up its anxious warning song.

'Is it always sunny like this?' Maeve said.

'Nearly always.'

In the kitchen he swung open the refrigerator door and pointed to the shelves. 'Is there anything there you fancy?'

'Yummy,' said she. 'I'm famished.'

He watched as she leaned into the refrigerator, investigating, moving jars aside. He thought of Father Kinneally opening the refrigerator and eating a grape. It seemed ridiculous for ghosts to be hungry. But then, he thought, the real Maeve is not a ghost; she is alive at this very moment in the town of Dundalk in

Ireland, probably driving her Mini to the parochial school to pick up two of her four children. 'Maeve,' he said. 'You know, you're not really famished.'

She turned and looked at him. She had taken a plum from the refrigerator and now bit into it. 'Why's that?' she asked.

'Because the real you is not here. The real you is in Ireland, married, forty-three years old, four kids, the wife of Dr Dan Coyle. This you is just a figment of my imagination.'

Maeve sucked on the plum, masticated it, and discreetly spit the stone into her palm. 'People like you,' she said. 'People who don't believe in anything that they can't see proven before their own eyes. That's a sort of stupidity, you know.'

'So I'm stupider than you are because I am unable to believe in hellfire and indulgences and saints appearing to peasants in French villages and relics of the true Cross, oozing blood to order?'

'Yes, all that,' Maeve said equably. 'I'm sorry. I suppose stupidity is too strong a word. But you will admit, Fergus, it makes you sort of limited.'

'Limited? I'm the one in this family who writes books and makes up stories. I'm the one who imagines you there, eating that plum right now. At the moment, you're my invention.'

'Would you listen to the wee tin god?' Maeve said. 'Hey, can I have some of this cheese?'

'Go ahead.'

'All right.' Maeve unwrapped a round of Bel Paese. 'Have you ever thought of it this way? If you don't believe in an afterlife – and you say you don't – then, if you died this minute, I would cease to exist. For you. In that sense. I'm your invention. But, in fact, I would still exist. Heaven depends on more than your belief in it.'

'Look, let's drop this,' Fergus said. 'I'm not in the least bit interested in the question of an afterlife.'

'No?' Maeve smiled in her irritating way. 'Then why do you worry about your so-called literary reputation? I'll tell you why. Because, in your case, it's a substitute for belief.'

'That doesn't make sense.'

'Doesn't it?' Maeve said. 'As a Catholic, you were brought

up to believe in a life after death. But you can't believe in it. So you invent a substitute. You start worrying about your reputation outliving you. Your work becomes your chance to cheat the grave. That's a very attractive thought, particularly for ex-Catholics. That's why you care so much about your literary status.'

'Nonsense,' Fergus said irritably.

'How can you be sure? Your trouble is, you can't be sure of anything. You have no laws, no rules, no spiritual life at all. You have to make up your own rules of conduct. You have to become your own wee ruler, and found your own wee religion. You are your own god.'

'Well,' Fergus said. 'Tit for tat, then. Are you sure there's a life after death? Is any believer really sure?'

Maeve looked at him. 'Can *you* tell me right this minute if there is a life here on earth? Can you tell me if I'm your dream or if you are my dream?'

'*Your* dream?'

'Yes.'

'Ah!' said Fergus. He felt he had won the argument. 'Hold on a minute. You have to be my dream. Because, otherwise, why do I see you standing there, sixteen years old, when in real life you must be – what – forty-three?'

'Forty-two,' Maeve said.

'Well, then?'

But Maeve smiled as though she knew something he didn't. She bit into the piece of cheese.

'So you are my dream,' Fergus said decisively.

'You could just as well be my dream,' Maeve said.

'But here, in California? I'm *living* here, you're not.'

'That's not the point,' Maeve said.

'Well, what *is* the point? Why have all of you appeared to me today?'

Maeve looked at the round of cheese, pretending interest in its label.

'Am I going mad, is that it?'

Maeve laughed. 'Mad?'

'Then it's not that?'

Maeve looked at him, no longer amused. 'Look, Fergus. Don't

you realize I can't tell you anything? You have to find out for yourself.'

'Find out what?'

Maeve shook her head in slight exasperation, put the round of cheese back into the refrigerator, shut the refrigerator door, and walked towards the glass doors which led to the terrace.

'Maeve? Can't you give me a clue?'

Turning momentarily towards him, Maeve pulled the doors shut, closing him in. She looked at him, her face expressionless, and then, with no sign of farewell, turned and walked across the terrace towards the steps which led down among the banks of ice plants to the sandy beach. He watched her go, then looked beyond her at the waves. Down there, at the tide line, a small figure stood, surf-casting. Beside the fisherman was a plastic bucket and a camp chair. Retired men came here to fish: on weekdays at this time of year they were, usually, the only people on the beach. If Maeve continued on down towards the water, and if she were not a hallucination, the fisherman would notice her. Keeping his eye on Maeve, Fergus groped for and found the binoculars which hung on a nail near the glass doors. Focusing the binoculars, he saw her standing at the edge of the ice plants, looking down at the bank of earth fill which spilled onto the sands of the beach. She put her foot on the earth fill, testing, then, risking it, half-ran, half-slid down to the safety of the sands below. Focusing on her face, Fergus saw her smile and pull off the barrette which held her hair in a bun. Her hair, caught by the wind, blew loose. She brushed it back from her eyes, and then, raising her head as people do when they smell the sea, began to walk towards the waves.

Swinging the binoculars to the right, Fergus refocused on the fisherman. An old man, from his stance, he had two fishing rods, one of which he held, positioning himself some twenty feet from the waves, the second rod, to his left, stuck into a pole holder, its invisible line holding it taut as a pennant, the bait caught in the heavy swell of sea far out beyond the breaking surf. Lowering the glasses, Fergus saw the scene in panorama: Maeve's small figure approaching the waves and the fisherman; the fisherman looking out to sea, unaware of her approach.

Maeve paused and removed her shoes, holding them in her right hand, as, her schoolgirl tunic blowing about her black-stockinged thighs, she walked splay-footed, kicking up sand for amusement. She was about a hundred feet from the fisherman when, tugging on his line, he half-turned towards her and, caught in that moment of turning, seemed to look at her. Fergus, hurriedly putting up the binoculars, tried to focus on the fisherman's face, but the fisherman had turned away once more and was busily reeling in his line.

Maeve, noticing the fisherman's sudden activity, began to hurry towards him. As she did, the fisherman jerked his rod high in the air, and a small fish gleamed in the sun on the end of the line. With a circular movement, scything his rod, the fisherman tossed the fish up onto the sands, clear of the waves. Maeve, running now, came up to where the fish lay. The fisherman, sticking his rod into a pole holder, went forward and, kneeling, freed the fish from its hook. Focusing, Fergus tried to frame the fisherman and Maeve together in his binoculars, but their heads were too far apart. He focused on Maeve.

She stood, not ten feet from the fisherman, looking down at him as he rose to his feet, carrying the fish. He walked towards his bucket and dropped the fish into it. Maeve seemed in contact with the fisherman, for he turned in her direction as though answering some question. The damned binoculars were not strong enough for Fergus to see lips moving, or the expressions on faces. They stood there, an oldish man in waders and a schoolgirl in navy tunic, not ten feet between them, both looking down at the bucket with the fish in it. The fisherman took bait from a smaller bucket, and kneeling again, began to rebait his line. Whereupon Maeve made a hand motion which might mean 'good-bye'. Good-bye it was, for she began to walk away, moving along the tide line, her stockinged feet only inches from the breaking waves.

The fisherman stood up, his line now baited, and returned to his camp chair. He cast. The line went far out beyond the breakers, went taut as the sea held the bait. The fisherman paid out the line a little, then, turning, sat in the camp chair, his legs extended, his heels digging into the sand.

Fergus, swivelling the binoculars, moved them to find Maeve, but should not have let her out of sight, for now the beach was bare. His glasses searched the line of the dunes to see if she was up there, but found no colour save grey sand and yellow grass. Turning, he raked the beach, searching for footprints, but there were myriad indentations and scattered marks on the sand. Suddenly decided, he hung the binoculars on the nail, went through the glass doors, across the terrace, and down the steps to the beach. He jumped from earth fill to sand, and then, a little self-conscious as to what role he should play with the fisherman, raised his arms to jogging stance. Running slowly, a man out for gentle exercise, he jogged towards the sea's edge, coming closer to the fisherman, rehearsing: 'Hello, getting any fish? Say, by the way, did you see a girl pass by a few minutes ago? My sister?' Something like that.

As he came up on the fisherman, the fisherman turned and looked in his direction. The fisherman wore a narrow-brimmed canvas hat and dark glasses and was not as old as Fergus had thought. Jogging, out of breath, Fergus ran down to meet the waves, then, veering right, walking, drew close to the camp chair. The fisherman smiled under his dark shades, a smile of greeting. 'Morning,' Fergus called. 'Getting any fish?'

The fisherman shrugged. Deprecating.

'Well, I see you got a couple,' Fergus shouted, looking into the bucket. He looked back at the fisherman. The fisherman nodded. Deprecating.

'By the way. Did you see a girl down here a few minutes ago?'

'Hah?' the fisherman asked. He removed his dark glasses and peered at Fergus. He was Oriental. Disappointment dropped on Fergus. Maybe the man did not speak much English?

'What's that?' the fisherman said.

'A girl, a school kid. Came by here a little while back?'

'Yes, one-two girls here,' the fisherman said. He put his dark shades on again. 'You lookin' for girl?'

'Yes,' Fergus said. 'The girl who was talking to you a little while ago. I wonder where she went.' Pantomiming his search, he turned and peered up at the line of dunes. The fisherman, swivelling in his camp chair, also looked back at the dunes. His head was shaped like a turtle's, his neck lined and seamed, his skin heavily tanned.

'A young girl,' Fergus said. 'Navy dress and black stockings?'

'I don't see her,' the fisherman said, looking.

'But you did see her. You know the one I mean? She came up when you caught that last fish?'

'No, sir, don't see her,' the fisherman said. He got out of the camp chair and took the second fishing rod out of its holder. 'Nice day,' he said. He gave a small Oriental nod as though dismissing Fergus. He walked towards the waves, entering the surf, his waders making a flapping movement. Fergus watched as the fisherman cast again, moving knee-high among the breaking waves. Then Fergus turned away, a lonely jogger, and ran back up the beach, jogging. He reached the bank of earth fill and scrambled up onto the steps which led to the house. Above him the house sat in the sun. Empty, quiet. He looked at his watch. It was after two. He went up, panting.

There was no Lincoln Continental in the driveway. Relieved, Fergus turned back, went into the house, and found some instant Kaffee Haag which he had bought in case Boweri ever paid him a visit. Boweri drank only Kaffee Haag. For his heart, he told Fergus. Although, come to think of it (and especially coming from Boweri), this did not necessarily imply that there was anything wrong with Boweri's heart. Fergus put the Kaffee Haag on a tray and arranged coffee cups, sugar bowl, and cream jug. Boweri used words as other men use handshakes: they were a form of polite contact, a convenience, not at all indicative of what he really felt or thought. And as far as I am concerned, Fergus surmised, Boweri probably thinks of me as a very simple person, a sort of peasant. I am a writer. I have only one persona, whereas he has multiple corporate and personal identities. He has said, at various times, that he is half-Irish. 'I had an old Tammany boss grandfather on my mother's side, name of Patrick O'Shea.' That he is Hungarian. 'And with a Hungarian for a friend, you don't need an enemy.' That he is Dutch. 'My name, you know, that's from the Bowery, New York Dutch stock, that makes me, you know, an old-line family bum.' That he has Negro blood. 'I tell you, I know what it's like to be a Black Panther. My grandfather on my mother's side, old Joe Rainbow, he was a full-blood Cree. And his wife was a coloured woman, she was a great human being, they tell me. So I'm part nigger, you understand.'

What *was* known for certain about Boweri was that he had been listed in a *Fortune* magazine survey as one of the one hundred richest men in the United States. Primarily he's a financial wizard, Fergus's literary agent said, the first time he mentioned Boweri's name, showing Fergus a letter written on heavy rag bond paper, headed 'Boweri Enterprises', with a Los Angeles address, a letter which stated that Mr Bernard Boweri would be interested in meeting your client Mr Fergus Fadden and for that purpose wished to invite Mr Fadden to spend three days in Los Angeles, offering first-class air travel and accommodation and an honorarium of two hundred dollars a day for each day including travel time in order that Mr Boweri might discuss with Mr Fadden a project connected with the possible purchase of the film rights to Mr Fadden's second novel. The letter went on to say that Mr Boweri was a great admirer of Mr Fadden's writing and that Mr Boweri hoped very much that Mr Fadden would accept the invitation. The letter had been signed, not by Boweri, but, for him, by his secretary. 'No,' said Fergus's literary agent. 'As far as I can find out, he's not an ordinary Hollywood producer, he's a millionaire who dabbles in movies as he dabbles in lots of businesses. He's one of this new breed. The conglomerate wizards.' How easy it was to rationalize that first taste of corruption, Fergus remembered, by saying that Boweri was no ordinary film producer. And that, if one had never been to Los Angeles, here was a perfect chance to pay a flying visit and be paid for it. Besides, Fergus desperately needed money. His ex-wife's demands were, as his lawyer put it, grim.

A conglomerate wizard. Fergus picked up the tray with the Kaffee Haag and carried it into the living room, remembering his false first meeting when he got off the plane from New York, walked into the Los Angeles airlines building, and there, coming to greet him, was a big man in a black silk shantung suit who said, 'Mr Fadden?' Eagerly, Fergus answered: 'Mr Boweri?', then saw that the man had a chauffeur's cap in his left hand. 'I'm Hank,' the man said, then led Fergus outside to an air-conditioned Lincoln Continental and drove him to the Bel Air Hotel. Later, Fergus found out that Hank had been Boweri's chauffeur for twelve years, and in that time, thanks to his employer's investment tips, Hank had become rich in his own right. By now Hank had managed to save enough to make a down payment on an apartment building in Long Beach. On his days off, this chauffeur drove a Lincoln Continental of his own. It was the current model, and it was air-conditioned. But he was still Boweri's servant. It was worth his while.

Perhaps it was that first glimpse of a California where the servants seemed like masters (and where any man might become rich, simply by being privy to a wizard's advice) which predisposed Fergus to the deferential mood he found himself in that evening when Hank picked him up again and drove him from the hotel to Boweri's Bel-Air mansion, the limousine moving with four-hundred-horsepower quiet through wrought-iron gates, past formal Spanish gardens and tree-shaded *paseos*, towards what looked suspiciously like the Royal Palace in Madrid. The house alone was worth half a million dollars, Hank informed him, a statistic Fergus was willing to believe, as a black manservant opened the front door to him, revealing a hall, large as a public concourse, through which, coming to greet him, immense and sinister, walking under a fresco honouring the Mexican God of Death, was Bernard Boweri. 'I warn you,' were Boweri's first words. 'I am your fan. I read both your books, and I love them. It's an honour to meet you, believe me.'

A lie, Fergus remembered, the first words Boweri ever spoke to me were a lie designed to make me lower my guard. Then Boweri put his arm around my shoulders and walked me down the corridor. His suit was dark and conventional, but his shoes were startling: red velvet slippers with a gold-threaded monogram on each instep. *BB*. He used a heavy perfume. On his right hand was a large emerald ring.

They entered a large library. Fergus noticed a beautifully

bound set of the Harvard Classics just inside the entrance and stopped, momentarily, to look at the book spines. 'I like sets of books,' Boweri said. 'Look over there. That's the entire Modern Library. When a new book comes out in the series, Bennett Cerf just sends it along. And look. That's every fiction selection of the Book of the Month Club, since World War Two. A year ago, I took a rapid-reading course. I liked it so much that for kicks I bought the company that sells the course. I put some money in, and since then it's doubled its growth rate. I like to do things that are worthwhile. Cultural things, you know?'

Boweri pressed his index finger against the spine of a *Palgrave's Golden Treasury of Poetry*. A wall of books moved, to reveal, behind them, a three-hundred-bottle bar. 'How's about a martini?' Boweri asked, picking up a martini jug which was at once transformed into child size in his huge hand. Stirring gin into the jug, he seemed to notice something over Fergus's shoulder. 'Ah,' said he. 'Here she is. Melia, my bride.'

Through the opened doors of the library Fergus saw an antebellum staircase, coming down which, her hand on the rail, was a tall blonde woman in a red velvet evening gown, wearing a many-tiered necklace of Peruvian silver. Fergus looked back at Boweri, who winked and said, 'Melia is uninhibited. I mean, in bed.'

She came up to Fergus, smiling as though she had heard what was said. She offered her hand. 'I've heard great things about you. But I'm honest, do you mind?'

Fergus, embarrassed, said he did not mind. Whereupon she said, 'I got to confess to you. I haven't read your books. Is that awful?'

'She never reads books,' Boweri said. 'You should worry.'

'Look who's talking,' Melia said. She linked her arm in Fergus's arm. 'My husband read that book of yours in half an hour. How can anybody read a book in half an hour?'

'I read it in an hour and a half,' Boweri corrected her. 'Two hundred pages an hour is normal in my reading course.'

'The thing about Bernie,' Melia said, 'is he's a liar.'

'That's business,' Boweri said. 'In business you buy cheap and sell dear. So already you are telling lies. I only wish I were a creator like you, Mr Fadden. I do! Imagine being responsible only to myself. The freedom. Me, maybe two thousand employees depend on me for their jobs. I am a slave to people. If I died tomorrow, I tell you, there'd be sixteen companies in some sort of trouble.'

Melia picked up a martini and smiled at Fergus. 'No man is indispensable,' she said, and winked. Fergus found himself blushing. He avoided her knowing eye and looked past the fake bookshelves of the bar, to real bookshelves, bookshelves which, in this part of the room, contained row upon row of titles such as *Placer Mining in Early Oregon*, *A New Theory of Molecular Structures*, *Lasers in Industrial Practice*, *Growth Stocks Versus Bonds*, *Depletion Allowances: The Senate Findings*, *Computer Retrieval Systems: A Study*, all of them subjects beyond his competence. And then, for the first time, it began to nag at him as it did so often in the ensuing months: perhaps Boweri's gaucheries and philistinisms, perhaps even Melia's come-hither behaviour, perhaps all was stage-managed, a trick to make Boweri's opponents feel over confident. Perhaps Boweri was, in reality, infinitely more intelligent than Fergus? With Boweri it was hard to know. Words did not help. Motives were concealed.

Now, remembering this, Fergus stared at the coffee tray, put a teaspoon beside Boweri's cup, then rose, thinking to fill the electric kettle with water, ready for boiling. As he did, he heard a familiar chuckle. Standing in the living-room doorway, Boweri: immense and sinister in a double-breasted ice-cream suit, wearing a royal blue shirt, fastened at the neck by an Apache scarf of vivid orange and black silk, his feet sockless in white alpargatas. Was this, too, a hallucination conjured up in the same way as Fergus's dead parents?

'You were thinking of me, weren't you?' Boweri said, chuckling.

'How did you know?'

'The Kaffee Haag on that tray. That's for me, right? Yes, that's sweet. Very sweet of you. Listen, I apologize for walking in like this, but I saw you through the window, sitting there, maybe in the middle of some creative thinking, and the door was open, and so I walked in. Excuse me. I am a vulgar man. My mother should have taught me to knock, but Fergie, you are looking at a man who never had a mother. A real son-of-a-bitch.'

But Fergus was not listening to this. He saw Boweri in his ice-cream suit, royal blue shirt, orange and black scarf, white alpargatas. He saw Boweri laugh at his own joke, heard the stress of his breathing, even noticed a small pulse beating in Boweri's temple. Yet there was seemingly no difference in the reality of Boweri, who could be here in this place at this time, and those others, who could not. Thus, a new anxiety was added to the day. From now on, how would he know who was real?

'Beautiful,' said Boweri, moving towards the glass doors to stare like stout Cortes on the Pacific. 'Peace, you got peace here. No people, no interruptions. Privacy. Yes, a writer's dream. I like it. Did you rent it by the month or by the year?'

'For the winter.'

'Big place, by the look of it.'

'Not really.'

'You get crowds on this beach, weekends?'

'No.'

'You should buy yourself a piece of land up here,' Boweri said. 'It's empty, no people, but in ten, fifteen years, this beach will be all high-rise apartments. Worth a lot of money.'

'I suppose so.'

'Listen, forgive me, I'm a vulgar person, but I just love to look at how other people live. Give me the tour, would you?'

Surprised (Boweri had never before evinced interest in any surroundings), Fergus rose and led him down the brick-tiled corridor.

'This is the room where I work.'

'I see. I interrupted you?'

'No, no.'

They went out into the hall. They entered the spare bedroom. The bed was made up, and there was a set of guest towels laid out on it. Fergus had not known this.

'You have guests?' Boweri asked.

'No. Not really. Wait! My girl friend's mother is coming for the weekend. My God, I forgot all about it!'

'And this is another bedroom?' Boweri asked, as they left the bedroom and went out into the corridor. Boweri pointed to the master bedroom, which Fergus shared with Dani. 'Three bedrooms, right? One of which you use as a workroom?'

'Yes.'

Boweri stopped. 'You got a bathroom attached, in there?' he asked, still pointing to the master bedroom.

'Yes.'

'Mind if I use it?'

'No, go ahead.'

Fergus waited outside the master bedroom, feeling awkward as he watched Boweri enter the room and shut himself in the connecting bathroom. The toilet flushed noisily. Water ran in the sink. Boweri re-emerged, smiling, holding up a pair of Dani's pink panty briefs. 'I should have said the little girls' room. I found this sitting on the john.'

Fergus took the pants and dropped them on the bed.

'Yes, it's a great little hideaway,' Boweri said. 'You done good, like a writer should. Let's go out on your terrace and have a little talk.'

On the terrace, Boweri refused a chair. 'I been sitting all day.' He stood with his back to Fergus and stared down at the beach. The fisherman was still there, surf-casting in the waves. 'Fishing,' Boweri said, 'is something I never could see. No kick, you know?' He stood, silent, for several moments. Then, portentously, he turned towards Fergus. 'Norman's gone to New York. He's unhappy. Frankly, Fergie, Norman is very disappointed.'

'Is he?' Fergus said, hoping he sounded cold.

'I told him, go,' Boweri said. 'Go to New York, try a change of scene for a few days. I'll speak to Fergie, I said. I bow to no one in my respect for Norman's talent. But face it, there is Norman Redshields the director and Norman Redshields the angry human being. I didn't want you to deal with a person who was not the director. Me, *amigo*, that's different. I don't get mad. Maybe it's a fault, who knows? But in a creative project where creative people are concerned, someone must produce. Someone must keep his cool. Right?'

'I assume,' Fergus said, 'Norman isn't pleased with the revisions I made?'

Boweri turned away, staring once more at the Pacific. 'Satisfied, not satisfied? Let's put it this way. There are some beautiful things in what you gave us. Some beautiful moments. But finally – *fin-ally* – we do not yet have a motion picture.'

'Look,' Fergus said. 'I made all the changes I felt I could make. I did the work in good faith. I sent it in to you people, and this is the first word I've heard from you in three weeks.'

'Frankly, Norman was too upset to call you.'

'Why was he upset?' Fergus asked. 'I was the one who should be upset. I had to make the changes.'

Boweri smiled and walked towards the egg chair. There was no question of his sitting in it: he was much too large. He pushed the egg chair gently, making it swing on its chain. 'But there were changes you *didn't* make,' he said. 'We need a lot more revisions.'

'I explained to you in my letter. I can't change the ending, it would be ridiculous.'

The egg chair came back from its swing, a second time. Boweri caught and held it. Smiling, he turned towards Fergus. '*Amigo*,' said Boweri, 'you're pushing me.'

'I'm not pushing anyone. I don't know why you bought my book if you don't think it should end that way.'

'Fergus,' Boweri said. 'Be reasonable. I wouldn't want to have to hire another writer. Another writer couldn't bring to this material the special qualities you brought to the book. The situation is special. I need your help.'

'I'm sorry. I'm not trying to be difficult.'

'But you are!' Boweri said, smiling. 'Yes, you are.'

'Redshields is the one who's being difficult.'

Boweri sighed. He released the egg chair, then walked over to a chaise longue. He inspected the chaise longue, and deciding it could take him, lay down on it, prone, looking up at the sky. His left hand reached for and cradled the great soft bulge of his genitals. 'Fergie,' he said, 'let me explain something. There is a standard clause. Nobody wrote it in special for you, it's in every contract, but it says we have the right to terminate the agreement with you in the event you do something which will bring you into public disrepute, contempt, scorn, ridicule, or that will tend to shock or offend the community, public morals or decency, or prejudice the employer – that's us – or the motion-picture industry in general. End of quote.'

'What are you talking about?' Fergus asked, although, suddenly sick, he felt he knew.

'Do I have to spell it out?'

'Well, yes, I think you do.'

'Okay,' said Boweri. 'Let's face it, you are in a very soft position here, *amigo*. You're living as man and wife out here on the beach with a little broad almost young enough to be your daughter. Meantime, your wife has a court action against you back East. You are a person whose name is known to a certain public, a scandal about you might just get in the newspapers. That could hurt our picture.'

'But that's ridiculous. And you know it.'

'Look,' Boweri said, 'who's complaining? Not me. I mention it – let me level with you – I mention it just to show that I'm not threatening you. But *you* are threatening me.'

'Me?' Fergus said.

'Yes, you, *amigo*. You are threatening the picture. You've got to give us an ending.'

'You have an ending.'

'With the ending you gave us, we can't make the picture. I keep telling you we need some hope. Some little lift so's the audience can walk out, they don't want to commit suicide. Now, nobody's leaning on you, Fergie, I don't want you to think that. I'm not looking for trouble, believe me. I am excited about the project, and I know you are too. Like always. And I know it's going to work, Fergie. We are going to have a picture we will all be proud of. Right?'

He is not an illusion, Fergus thought.

Boweri, coming up from his prone position, Lazarus arising from the grave, swung his legs over the edge of the chaise longue and sat, benign, smiling at Fergus. 'You think about it,' he said.

'I've thought about it –'

'Wait, wait, don't say anything. Let me explain you the situation. Norman wants to hire another writer. Tomorrow, he has lunch with a very fine writer. You dig? He wants to go with this guy. I told him, Norman, wait. I'm going to make a special trip today, I make it my business to talk to Fergus. Fergus is the best man we can have. I told him that. I said, Norman, I'm going to speak to Fergus and let him think about it. You call me tomorrow morning. I'll have an answer from Fergus. So, Fergus, please – think!'

'I've thought about it. I'm not going to make those changes.'

'*Amigo!*' Boweri said. He stood up, smiling, surprisingly light on his small feet. 'Now, listen, *amigo*,' he said. '*Somebody's* going to change that ending. *Believe* me. It might as well be you. You got personal troubles, you need money, you got the talent. Just think about it. If you change your mind, you call me tonight. I'll be home, okay?'

Fergus said nothing. Smiling, Boweri turned once more towards the sea, yawned, stretched, then consulted his gold Rolex Oyster wristwatch. 'Let's go to the races someday, soon, huh? I'll bring Melia, you bring this kid, whatshername?' He waited.

Fergus did not answer.

'Dani,' Boweri said, smiling. 'Short for Danielle, huh? Danielle Sinclair.'

How did he know her last name? Fergus wondered, but why wonder. There were ways. He followed Boweri around the side of the house. A green Lincoln Continental waited. Hank, the chauffeur, got out and opened the rear door.

'Hi there, Mr Fadden.'

'Hello, Hank.'

Boweri, yawning again, turned and laid plump hands on Fergus's shoulders, a bishop's gesture, a blessing. 'Great seeing you, Fergie. You'll call me tonight, okay? Don't forget. It's going to be a very exciting picture.'

Willing Fergus to say nothing at this time. Releasing him. Turning, light on his small feet, moving with one swift bound into the back seat of the limousine. Hank shut the door; it closed with a rich, satisfying clunk.

'Great day, huh?' Hank said to Fergus.

'Yes. Sure is.'

Snake smooth, the Lincoln curved around the driveway and, silent, climbed the hill. Stopped momentarily at the entrance to Pacific Coast Highway, then slid like a bullet into the breech of traffic. Gone. Fergus turned and went into the house. It was over; they would get someone else: he would not be paid what was owed him. He was in no position to sue. He would have to find some other way to raise money for his alimony and the divorce. He walked through the house and back out onto the terrace facing the sea. Rage weakened him, making him dizzy, his vision blurring as he stared down at the shore. Rage at his wife, at her vengeance, her lies, at her refusal to let him see his daughter, at her lawyers, the detective agencies she had hired, her impossible demands, which had driven him out to this Pacific Coast. What if tonight he just disappeared? It would be so easy to vanish. Twenty miles north of here was the perfect town: Oxnard, Ventura County, California. A living tomb, a Navy missile base, home of the Pacific Seabees, and an Air Force installation, with lemon groves, rail yards, Mexican fruit pickers, Japanese vegetable farmers, a wasteland of shopping centres, tract houses, trailer camps, marinas, a town filled with the migrant Okies of the seventies, their licence plates a gazetteer from the main streets and back roads of Louisiana, Texas, Florida, Missouri, Montana, Illinois, a staging ground for strangers, a town where you would never in twenty years meet anyone you had known. Hidden in Oxnard, he would send out money to feed and clothe his daughter, mailing it in unmarked envelopes from postal drops in other American states. But his wife, his enemy, would hunt for him in vain, her detectives roaming the Western states, even tracking back to Europe, to the cities he had once known, proliferating at all times those gumshoe bills of one hundred dollars and up *per diem*. He smiled at the sea. Not finding him, she would have to pay those bills. And her lawyers' bills. And her charge accounts. Subterranean, he would hide for five years, silent, unfindable, until she, forced to abandon her search, must divorce him and marry a new protector. Five years of no identity, driving an old Oldsmobile registered in his friend Dick Fowler's name, working as an anonymous checkout helper in Oxnard's Thrifty Drugstores, Pic 'N Saves, and Food-O-Marts, living in twenty-dollar-a-week rooming houses (those lay monasteries of our age), his nights spent in the monkish company of fellow drifters and loners, each man isolated with his thoughts as they gathered together in the rooming-house lobby to lounge on plastic-covered armchairs and watch television. Eating loner's meals in diners and cafeterias: pizza, spaghetti and meatballs, Swiss steak and french fries, with – yes! – on special occasions, Thanksgiving or Christmas, the Holiday Menu Special, Roast Tom Turkey with All the Trimmings, Plum Pudding and Hard Sauce, choice of juice or soup! At last, he would be one of those solitaries who had his Christmas pudding alone. And twice a week, as a treat, he would go to the movies, accepting uncritically the changes of programme provided by Oxnard movie managements. Five years of this: five years to write his *Notes from Underground*, his hermit's book. In all that time, no correspondence, no phone calls, no visits from or to friends. But what about Dani? My God, how could he have forgotten Dani! She stood, sudden in his mind, as in wild improvisation he scrambled to reassemble his fantasy with Dani as Temptation to his Saint Anthony. But Oxnard crumbled. Why should Dani be forced to live in seedy rooming houses, how could you ask her to share a hermit's existence, to retreat to some Matto Grosso industrial jungle, some tract house Arabia Deserta for five precious years of her young life? Ridiculous!

A Navy jet fighter, ripping through the sky, shattered the silence of the terrace. The egg chairs shook on their chains. The plane noise died, and as it did, Fergus, staring mindlessly at the ground, saw, with the excitement of a man who sights a jewel in the dirt, one small oval plum stone, a piece of chewed pith adhering to its edge. It lay, still damp, wedged in the interstice between two terrace bricks. Stooping, Fergus picked up the plum pit, felt its wetness in his palm. His sister Maeve had spit this plum pit into her hand, walked across the terrace, then, as one would, let the stone drop from her hand, once she was outside.

'Hallucinations cannot eat real plums.'

He had said it aloud, and suddenly, he laughed. Had he eaten a plum? No, he didn't even like plums, he bought them for Dani. Had Boweri? No. Dani, did she eat a plum before leaving this morning? No, she left by the front door, without coming out here. The only person who could have eaten this plum, the stone still wet with the half-chewed pith on it, was Maeve. So I am not going mad, he thought. Something happened here today, some-

thing phenomenal. No, more than phenomenal, for a pheno-
menon in the Kantian sense *could* be an illusion, but here, in my
hand I have empirical proof that these apparitions are not ordinary hallucinations. After all, what do my troubles with Boweri
matter, when weighed against this discovery? I *did* smell my
father's cigarette. I am holding in my hand the stone of a plum
which I *saw* Maeve eat. Smell, touch, sight. If I had touched
Maeve I would have felt her skin as though it were real. If these
are apparitions, and like some necromancer, I can conjure them
up? Cannot only see them, but can actually smell them, touch
them?

He did not even put his thought into words; it translated itself
from a pre-speech area of his brain into an instant materialization
of Mrs Findlater on the chaise longue at the far end of the terrace,
half-sitting, half-lying on the cushions, one foot touching the
brick terrace, the other raised, leg dangling, knee held cupped in
her hands and she smiling in that remembered, innocent, friend-
of-your-mother way, ignoring or innocent of the fact that her
skirt had fallen back so that he could see the top of her nylon
stockings, girdle straps, white thighs, pink, tight knickers.

As always in the past, he pretended not to look, yet looked,
photographing every detail of her holy of holies in the retina of
his memory, willing himself to retain every skin shade, every
positioning of fabric and flesh so that at night, while she lay in
bed in her house on Cornwallis Road with the dentist she was
married to, Fergus, in his own bed at home, would re-create this
vision of her sitting innocently on show, and, in his favourite
erotic fantasy, imagine that he sat beside her as, smiling, she took
his hand and placed it on her silky, stockinged thigh, letting him
slide his fingers up to touch her white skin, his fingers moving on
into the soft recesses of her inner thighs, and, almost invariably,
the thought of doing that was enough, his fantasy did not require
actual intercourse, but at the memory of her white thigh culmin-
ating in tight, pink knickers, he climaxed in a frantic jerking of
his penis under the bedclothes. Then, as the hot milky semen
cooled to clammy discomfort, he would begin his rosary of worries, first that Jim, in the other bed, had noticed the tent-pole
agitation under his blankets, then, that the anaemia the haematolo-

gist said he had begun to suffer from was caused by this nocturnal pollution, then, that anyone who spied on girls and women the way he did was mentally disturbed and at, say, twenty-four, his brain weakened, his memory gone, not able to concentrate, let alone study and pass exams, would be shipped off to end his days among the feeble-minded in Purdysburn Asylum. But often, even as he lay in this pool of post-masturbation guilt, he would become excited again, perhaps bringing to mind his very best view ever of Mrs Findlater, on that astonishing and terrifying afternoon when his mother asked him if he would go over to the Findlaters' house and clean out their garden shed because the dentist had a wrenched back and couldn't stoop. And she, Mrs Findlater, had wanted to ask Fergus to help, but was too shy. Shy? She? Fergus said at once that he would go, and when he got to the Findlater house, the dentist was out pulling teeth and she was alone. She asked if he would excuse her, for she was going to take a nice hot bath and afterward she would make the two of them some tea. When Fergus went outside to clear the mess from the garden shed, he noticed that the shed was directly facing the bathroom window, which was on the second floor of the house.

At once, not Fergus but the sex maniac who hid inside him began, without a qualm, to climb up on the roof of the shed, then lay prone for a good ten minutes, ignoring Fergus's warnings that anyone on an upper floor of any of these houses had only to look out a window and it would be farewell Fadden. But the sex maniac kept his eyes fixed on the partly opened window of the bathroom. He could see a clear space between the windowsill and the frosted windowpane, and watched, unblinking, until suddenly she was in the bathroom, in her bathrobe, moving out of sight, then reappearing completely naked, the bottom part of her moving about, not twenty feet from his eyes, showing herself both front and rear, until, suddenly, terrifyingly, she got into the bathtub, lowering herself until her head came into view at his eye level, while he, in panic, dragged himself backward on his belly to slide (Satan the Snake in the Garden of Eden) down off the roof into a nettle bush, which mottled his hands with a rash of white, painful, lumpish stings. Twenty minutes later, still in a funk, his hands still stinging, he heard her call out. Would he come in a minute? Went in, in panic, for if she had seen him up there on the roof, just what could he say? There was no excuse that would save him. But when he entered the house, she was sitting all dressed up, her hair done, presiding over a tea tray with buttered cream crackers and a jam roll on it, and he knew she had not seen him, she was innocent of the fact that he, Fergus Fadden, had feasted his eyes on her most secret parts. He knew her, knew all of her, and she was innocent of this filthy knowledge of his, a fact which when he thought of it then, and in all subsequent meetings with her, filled him with a poignant yet erotic sensation of having demonically possessed her. On Sunday mornings he would sit in the Church of the Most Holy Redeemer, watching her as she knelt six benches ahead of him, her head bent submissively in the presence of her God, while kneeling beside her, cuckolded by Fergus's lascivious eyes, Conor (Lugs) Findlater, Doctor of Dental Surgery, read his missal and coughed his smoker's cough. Watching this Holy Family at prayer, Fergus would sometimes receive instant erection, and suddenly, satanically, in God's house, would begin to recite to himself a Marian litany of her delights, tower of ivory, house of gold, ark of the covenant, gate of heaven, morning star, assigning to each invocation some naked sight, the glimpse of her full, dark-nippled breasts, her smooth, girlish belly, her bottom, pink and spankable, and the ark of the covenant itself, that V of downy dark hair he had seen with his eyes, the holy of holies itself.

And now, in California, remembering those shameful delicious Black Masses of his imagination, he looked again at her, this woman whom he, a necromancer, had conjured up from his adolescent past, a woman whose excitative quality could not be matched by any other female in the whole world, for she alone remained fixed in his boyhood fantasy, impregnably protected by the most delicious taboo: she was his mother's first cousin and her best friend. Her husband, the dentist, was actually Fergus's godfather. And remembering this, as she sat opposite him on the chaise longue on this sunlit terrace, smiling, innocently exposing her limbs, materialized again to do his bidding, his *creature*, he felt the calves of his legs stiffen and the tendons of his heels commence trembling, and sat down on a deck chair in the sunlight, smiling at her uncertainly, reduced to adolescent dumb-tongue as she asked: 'Well, Fergus, and what have *you* been doing with yourself lately?'

'Oh, nothing much,' he mumbled. Her first name was Edna, and he had always called her Edna in his mind but never to her face, of course, although she had urged him to do so.

She leaned back, hands still cupping her knee, giving him the most fantastic peep show, her floral print dress falling back from her upraised leg, revealing the whole soft, beautiful white underside of her thigh, the curve of her bum in tight pink knickers, and his heart, as of old, was so loud and urgent that he could not trust himself to speak. 'Con and I were at the Old Boys Association Dance,' she said. 'I looked for you there. Wasn't Con after you to join the association?'

Con was the dentist.

'He was,' Fergus said, 'but there's not much point. I mean, you know, living in California.'

The conversation, he reflected, was as ridiculous as his conversations with her in the past. He had never known what he was saying. And now, remembering that Con Findlater was dead these nine years, he wondered what on earth had made her say what she'd just said. But then, he had often suspected she had not known what she said to him. Perhaps, after all, there *had* been some mutual attraction? Emboldened, Fergus moved his deck chair closer, and, emboldened, took another furtive look at the curve of her lovely white thigh.

'And how is your mother keeping?'

'She's dead,' Fergus said.

'Oh, so she is. She was a saint of God, your mother was. I was her best friend, you know.'

'Yes.'

'You were a great family. Such fun to visit.'

She smiled, reminiscent, and looked down at the beach. The fisherman was still there, surf-casting. 'Yes, the Fadden family,' she said. 'Your father, such a fine man. And you, Fergus, isn't it simply super what's happened to you? Well known in America as a journalist, and now an author. Would you believe it, the lad who used to come and see us there on the Cornwallis Road. I always thought you were clever, though. You used to contradict me about the books I liked, do you remember?' She laughed girlishly. 'Oh, you used to tell me off, all right.'

'I always liked *you*,' Fergus said, in what he hoped was a double-entendre manner.

'Did you? Well, I'd never have guessed it.'

'I mean, I always thought you were very pretty. I mean, you *are* very pretty.'

'Oh, no!' said she. 'Your mother was right about you. Fergus of the golden tongue, she called you.'

'My mother?'

'Yes, we were talking one time long ago about you and your brother, and I said you were both nice boys but that Jim was the shy one. And your mother said you were the talker. "Fergus of the golden tongue," she said, and I remember I said, "Mark my words," I said, "that fellow will break hearts a few years from now." Yes. Those are the very words I used.' Mrs Findlater laughed, leaning back, revealing herself all the way up to the waistband of her knickers.

He put his hand on her bare thigh. He stared into her face. She laughed, leaning back. It was as though he had not touched her. He was doing what he had always wanted and she exactly what, in his adolescence, he would have wished for most. She was pretending that nothing was happening. He moved his fingers over her soft flesh, lascivious, slow. 'Yes,' she said. 'Con and I were talking about you just the other day. Con read that article about your book in *Time* magazine and showed it to me, and I said, "Well, Con," I said, "I remember years ago his mother saying that Fergus has a golden tongue." '

Babbling on the way she had always babbled on, but now, what a difference! She wasn't sitting in her own sitting room in a chintz-covered chair, she was here, lying full length on this chaise longue, smiling, staring dreamily up at the bougainvillea bush while he, with both his hands pushed up into the tight silky legs of her knickers, had her in his power; she would not say a word, no matter what he did, even if he took her knickers down. 'Yes, and Con said *he* remembered that your father won a gold medal in English. So Con said. Did he?'

'Did he what?'

'Win a gold medal in English. Con said he did.'

'Yes, he did.'

She nodded and smiled, still looking up at the flowering bush. 'Then Con was right. Anyway, Con said you took it, I mean your writing ability, you took it from your father's side of the family.'

Bold, trembling, he pushed her skirt up over the waistband of her knickers. He began to ease the knickers down.

'But I said, never mind his father's side of the family, let me tell you there's no one has a way of telling a story the way Julia Fadden has. No one.'

As she said this last 'no one' she obligingly raised her bottom up off the chaise longue to let him slide her knickers all the way down to her knees. 'The Kearneys, your mother's family, they were all great storytellers. They were grand value.'

Fergus looked at her smooth white belly, his eyes fixed on that downy V of pubic hair he had seen years ago when he climbed on the roof of her garden shed. He reached out and slid his hands under the firm white globes of her bottom. 'And Danno Kearney, they called him, you must have heard your mother speak of him, your mother's uncle Dan, he used to be famous the length and breadth of Ireland as a *scannaiche*, a storyteller.'

Gripping those beauteous soft globes, and oh God, it was too quick, it was like all the times he had lain in bed, about to do it to her in his mind, he never got further than the preliminaries, just holding her bare bum was enough. He released her hurriedly, caught hold of his spending stiff member, pulling it out of his trousers, jerking it. For a moment she looked in his direction, but gave no sign that she had noticed. Negligently, she shifted on the chaise longue. 'Yes, he came from Dungannon, he used to come into the town on fair days, and when the sales were over, the people would gather around him in a snug, and off he'd start with his yarns.'

Lying there on the chaise longue with her pants down, pretending she hadn't noticed him fiddling with his member. 'Did your mother never tell you about him?' she asked, and he found himself, as of old, flushed, guilty, shaking his head. 'Well, anyway,' she said. 'He was a great old fellow.' And then: 'Fergus, would you excuse me a moment? I have something I have to do.'

Sliding her legs off the chaise longue, rising to her feet, pretending to settle her skirt but, in reality, hitching up the pink knickers which were down about her knees, turning her back to him, Edna Findlater, his first great lust, walking away across the terrace, disappearing behind the bougainvillea bushes. Probably going back there to tell his mother what he had done. And as always, post-masturbation, it was *bonjour tristesse*. To think that if you were vouchsafed the chance to bring some one person back from your past, he would seek, not someone who would contribute to his happiness, his enlightenment, or even his wealth, but would at once plump for seeing Edna Findlater with her knickers down and coming in his hand as of old. It was, he realized, the fulfilment of that self-hating self-prophecy which at seventeen he believed to be the truth: namely that the one thing he lived for was self-abuse.

She reappeared from behind the bougainvillea bushes. Her face was grave. 'You're wanted,' she said, pointing to the glass doors which led to the living room. The doors were partly open. He could see people inside. 'Hurry yourself now,' said Edna Findlater. 'They're waiting for you.'

She had told his mother. That was the only thing he could think of as he rose and faced the doors. He looked at her, and of course she went straight in, hurrying to give testimony. What they did with boys who attacked their mothers' best friends was something he had once thought about a lot. In his case, knowing his parents, he had imagined they would want to hush it up as far as the outside world was concerned, but there would be one awful interview with the dentist himself, which might even end with the dentist being given permission by Fergus's parents to administer a thrashing. Maybe with a cane.

But he had been wrong. They were not going to hush it up. He stood, facing the partly opened doors. He could hear many voices – the courtroom buzz before the court is called to order. Two policemen emerged from the house, coming out to him, escorting him through the doors, each placing a hand on Fergus's elbow as though to steady him. They were not the large robot police of

Los Angeles, jackbooted, sun-visored, with shoulder flashes and white crash helmets, but stunted, red-faced wee men, stiff in black serge, with heavy black raincapes and big, black, beat-pounding boots. Each was belted into a leather-encased truncheon and a leather-holstered service revolver. Uniform caps with flat black birdbill peaks came down like a carapace over their noses; in the centre of each cap's forehead band was a small red-and-black badge, the insignia of the Royal Ulster Constabulary. 'Right y'are,' said one in clipped Ulster-Scots tones. 'Get over there, again' that wall.' Moving close as he spoke, dealing, under the shield of his raincape, a low blow to Fergus's privates, which caused Fergus's eyes to blur in pain so that the faces in the room beyond swam in a watery, out-of-focus mash. The second police-man spun him around to face the wall. A harsh Ulster voice called out over the mix of conversation in the room, 'Right now. Quiet there. Let's get started.'

Fergus, his eyes clearing, turned to peer, startled by the familiar in that voice. In the centre of the room, pale, skinny, a thick lock of hair falling over his right eye, looking young and foolish in an ill-advised suit of cheap Prince of Wales checks, with a badly tied polka-dot bow tie and a straight-stemmed pipe which he held, like a child playing a detective in a school play, the familiar of Fergus's first passport photograph pointed at Fergus, as though indicating to the others in the room the man he would one day become. Shocked, Fergus tried to see who those others were, but the policeman on his right at once took hold of his earlobe and jerked him around to face the wall. 'Start that gawkin' again,' the policeman warned, 'and I'll give it to you right atween the eyes.'

Filled with new fear, Fergus obeyed, smelling foul onion from the policeman's breath. He heard his younger self calling for order. 'Quiet, please, quiet! Now, what's the charge?'

'Public indecency,' a voice called.

'Molesting a woman!'

'No, no!' his young voice called. 'That's not the issue. The real charge is more serious. Quiet, please!'

There was quiet. His young voice said, 'First statement. This house yields to Patrick Donlon.'

Paddy Donlon's voice, the knowing voice of the pub: 'Right now. A man is what he does, not what he says he does.'

'Right, yes, okay, right, yes, that's right,' mingling voices shouted, amid a coughing, shuffling of feet, clearing of throats. Involuntarily, Fergus tried to look, but, arrested by the eye of his guard, was cautioned by that eye that this policeman was unholy eager to punish misdemeanor. Cowed, Fergus confronted the wall. 'All right,' said Paddy Donlon's voice. 'Let's take a look at his record.'

'Political position?' someone called.

'Well,' said his younger self. 'In my last year in school, and when I went on to university, I called myself a socialist.'

'Correction!'

'The floor yields to Conor Findlater, Doctor of Dental Surgery.'

'Pardon me, interrupting like this,' the dentist said. 'I hope this isn't telling tales out of school, and I hope you people know this is quite apart from his disgraceful conduct in connection with my Edna, but I remember very well that my good friend Monsignor Sean Clooney, Catholic chaplain in residence at Queen's University, gave it to me as his considered opinion that after hearing young Fadden debate in the students' union it was his judgement that this young fellow-me-lad was definitely a Red Communist!'

Behind Fergus's back the room went loud with laughter. 'Communist!' someone shouted. 'Oh, that Monsignor Clooney is a great judge of men!'

'Wait,' shouted another voice amid the yells of glee. 'Let himself tell us his real position.'

His younger self cleared his throat, self-importantly. 'In point of fact, I definitely admired the party. I had friends who were party members.'

Roars of dissent interrupted this confession.

'May I – *please!*' cried an American voice.

'The floor yields to Chaim Mandel.'

Mandel, Fergus's great friend in Greenwich Village, a contributor to New York literary-political reviews and an activist for both Old and New Left causes, was listened to now, by all, in respectful silence. 'He's got to be joking,' Mandel began. 'In point of fact, Fergus is in his late thirties and not only has he, to my certain knowledge, never joined a political party, he has never done a real day's work for any political cause.' Mandel laughed. 'Wait! He did spend two evenings with a former girl friend of mine, making her catechumenize him on the names of American presidents and some elementary dates in American history. This was to help in his application for American citizenship.'

'*American* citizenship?' someone shouted, as though repeating the punch line of a joke.

'Yield to Chaim Mandel!'

'The problem here,' said Mandel's voice, 'is that this man is not living in history. His work, such as it is, ignores the great issues of the age. His life is narcissistic: he is completely ensnared by the system. True, he has rejected his ethnic background and has denounced the class, race, and religion into which he was born. But to reject is not enough. Lacking a true foundation, he has fallen back on cliché: the romantic sacerdotal ethic of art for art's sake, which was already dead and buried forty years ago. And so, ultimately, made reckless by his rootlessness, he has been led, sheeplike, to the final solution. Hollywood!'

'Well put! Well said, Chaim!'

'A creative criticism!'

'Mandel's exegesis has elucidated the essence of the problem!'

'Ah, get away out of that! Sure your man Fadden isn't worth the argument. He's a flaming bloody fraud!' That was Harry Daley, he knew it was Harry Daley, everyone was a flaming fraud to Harry Daley.

'No, not a fraud,' Mandel summed up. 'Merely a victim of the dichotomy imposed by intellectual self-exile.'

'But he's not me!' his younger self cried. 'He's *him!* It's nothing to do with self-exile, it's to do with age! Somewhere along the line *he* began to believe that opinions were deeds. You all know how fond he is of lecturing people – explaining the British National Health scheme –'

Many began to chuckle.

'– Relating British Labour Party policy to the British class system, being comic about the fantasies of American Trotskyites and the paranoia of New York Stalinists in the fifties, giving his two-step lecture on the American manoeuvres in Guatemala, describing Russian tactics in Poland and his visits to Haiti and pre-Castro Cuba, oh, and don't forget the Middle East – remember Suez? Wait, I'll tell you about that. You might say Suez was the only time in his life that he set out to *do* something political instead of just talking about it. Yes. He was in London at the time of Suez, and one Sunday he went to Trafalgar Square, ostensibly to take part in a sit-down demonstration against Eden's policies.'

There was a sudden silence in the room. Someone coughed. 'But, in fact,' said his younger self, 'part of the reason he was lured down to Trafalgar Square was a set of newspaper photographs he had seen of a previous Sunday's sit-down demonstration in which pretty young girls were being carried off by the police, kicking, showing their thighs and their panties! And we all know how fond he is of that!'

'Yield the floor to Mrs Findlater!'

'No, wait!' yelled his younger self. 'I haven't finished yet. When he reached Trafalgar Square, he did not, in fact, sit down with the demonstrators, but stood, facing them, safe behind the police lines, looking up the girls' skirts as they were carried off.'

Again the room was loud with hateful laughter. 'If I can just explain –' Fergus began, attempting to turn around and face his accusers. But the policeman on his right held a fist to his nose.

'Wait!' said his younger self. 'What does he want to say?'

'What *can* he say?' yelled Harry Daley. 'Flaming bloody fraud!'

'Yield to the accused!'

The policeman lowered his fist. Fergus, turning, saw the room, blurred, a frieze of hostile faces, and in the centre, straight-stemmed pipe in hand, his younger self, that traitor.

'You'd tell that!' Fergus said, his voice thick with emotion. 'Don't you know that's a story about *you*, that story of Trafalgar Square?'

His younger self, hair falling over his right eye, smiled at him, a set smile of hate.

'God!' said Fergus. 'You'll do anything for an audience. Tell on anybody. Tell anything! Is nothing private to you?'

His young self smiled. 'I'm a writer.'

'A writer! What have you written, you –' Moving forward to strike, but both policemen punched simultaneously, one in the kidneys, one in the genitals. Coughing, gagging, Fergus was spun back to face the wall.

'Not only did he not act politically, he didn't even write anything political,' Dan Gavan's voice said.

'I'm not a political writer,' Fergus told the wall.

'True!' cried the Irish poet Hugh Gildea. 'He's not a political writer. Writing is the crux of this matter. He told me he didn't want to take an active part in politics because he believed the writer *engagé* was always a revolutionist *manqué*. And usually wound up as a writer *manqué* in the end. He cited several examples.'

'How can anybody take that position?' asked the knowing, back-of-the-pub voice of Paddy Donlon. 'How can anybody write fiction in this day and age and ignore what's happening in the world. Eh, lads?'

'I'm not ignoring –' Fergus began, but the policeman on his right jabbed him in the ribs.

'The dedicated-artist line,' said the voice of Isobel Montrose. 'When I met him in Paris ten years ago he was living in the Hotel Acropolis. He let me use his bathtub. I didn't have one. He liked to talk to me through the door while I was having a bath. Because I was a painter he didn't just use the dedicated-artist line to dodge his political responsibilities. It was useful in other ways. I remember him quoting Cyril Connolly that the pram in the hall is the enemy of art. His art *and* mine.'

'Och, aye,' shouted Dan Gavan, over laughter. 'Peeking through the doorjamb at you as he said it. And that other codology of your man Connolly, he was fond of quoting: "the only duty of a writer is to write a masterpiece!"'

'A masterpiece?' said an English voice. 'From a minor Irish writer?'

'Not major. No major works,' said an American voice.

'By major I suppose you mean a lot of pages?' Fergus heard himself shout.

'Just a Catholic writer!'

'I never was a Catholic writer!'

'Ex-Catholic. Irish. Same thing.'

'Genre writer!'

'Fluke!'

'Wait!' his younger self shouted, that harsh, anxious voice, louder than all the others in the room. There was silence. 'All right, now,' said his younger self, this time addressing Fergus directly. 'In politics you've always believed yourself to be liberal, at least. But, in fact, what side have you been on? What have you ever really done to help anybody or any cause, ever?'

Fergus, silent, stared at the wall. There must have been times, causes, he was sure of it.

'What about civil rights in Ulster?' Dan Gavan called.

'What could I do? I'm living here,' Fergus told the wall. 'I sent a letter of support and a cheque to Bernadette Devlin. I wrote that I admired what she had done.'

'Exactly. You sent a cheque. You always send a cheque. Apart from giving small sums of conscience money, you do nothing. You've concentrated on your writing, your pleasures, your own affairs. True or false?'

'Well, in a way it's true,' Fergus said. 'But –'

'But your justification would be the merit of your writing. You've written two books, some short stories, and many articles. Do you think posterity will read your work?'

Fergus was silent.

'Well?'

'Well, I mean, how would I know? That's not for me to say.'

'No? But you have said it. You've told quite a few girls that you're a genius.'

Behind Fergus's back the people in the room began to snigger.

'Just drunk talk,' Fergus said.

'*In vino veritas*,' said the voice of the dentist.

'Look, how does anyone know anything nowadays?' Fergus said weakly. 'I mean, with the world in the state it's in. There are no standards anymore.'

The sniggers fanned to laughter. 'Perfect!' cried Isobel Montrose. 'Blame the world situation!'

'No, no, this is serious,' said his younger self. 'Please?' The laughter diminished. 'Look,' said his younger self. 'I'm asking him a question, the most important question of his life. I'm asking you, Fergus Fadden, what have you accomplished? Do you realize that, at thirty-nine, you're already on the westward slope?'

'Washed up on a beach in California!' someone called out.

'You don't understand! I'm here for special reasons. I have to pay alimony –'

'Immoral bastard,' said the dentist. 'Always some excuse for his filthiness.'

'Pure selfishness,' said Isobel Montrose. 'Why should being a writer constitute an excuse?'

'*Vous êtes écrivain?*' It was the voice of Georges de Foresta, his former landlord at Tourettes. '*Un vrai? Un écrivain pour moi, c'est un homme exceptionnel.*'

'*Mais il y en a des écrivains, Georges,*' said the voice of Henriette, his girl. '*A Paris, presque tous les étrangers s'appellent écrivains. Des fumistes! Tous!*'

'Talent,' said an old, reedy voice. 'In the opinion of this reviewer, this book shows genuine talent.'

'But has he?' asked his younger self. 'Is he going to be read, say, fifty years from now?'

'In my opinion,' said Dan Gavan, 'not a chance.'

'But if he *has* any talent,' said Hugh Gildea, the poet, 'posterity won't give a hang for his private life or his political foolishness.'

'Who knows who history will absolve?' asked the voice of Chaim Mandel.

'And who cares?' said Dick Fowler's voice. 'That's, like, your generation, baby, that type thinking. It's now, it's today, baby, it's here. That's where it's at.'

'Just do your thing. Make love, not war. You'll be a long time dead,' cried a high unisex voice which Fergus often heard on local records.

'Yeah, yeah, yeah.'

'I paint,' said Isobel Montrose, 'because I want to paint. Who knows what will happen when we're dead?'

'Who flaming cares?' cried Harry Daley.

'I care,' said the voice of his younger self. 'Don't you see? He's my future.'

'Pray silence for a verdict!'

A judge spoke, his accent Scots, his tones measured, stern. 'Your future? Very well, my son. Look over there. Do you see that fool of a man standing there in a rented house in California, hearing voices, seeing ghosts, not knowing if he has taken leave of his senses? Take a look at him, laddie. That man there wi' his teeth loose in his jaws, combing his hair over his bald spot, telling himself he's in love wi' a lassie who's young enough to be his daughter!'

'But I'm not asking about his life, it's his writing I'm asking about!' cried his younger self, his voice panicky, imploring. The room went quiet. 'Please?' his younger self called. 'Someone take the floor? Isn't there an answer?'

Some person coughed. There was a moment of silence; then Fergus heard the footsteps of many people, the sound one hears when people get up to leave a church after a service, no voices, but a shuffling, scraping sound, chairs pulled back, the sound of a procession. On either side of Fergus, the policemen turned to look at each other, and then by unspoken agreement, drew back from the wall, leaving him standing there alone. There was a great stillness. Cautiously, he turned around. The room was empty as a church, a minute after its closing. He stood for a moment. Then he heard the sea.

Trembling, suddenly nauseated, he walked forward into the living room and sat down on the yellow sofa, his hands gripping his kneecaps. Tense, so tense he found himself nodding, his head jerking forward as though he had dozed off. He leaned back, holding his breath. And then he must have dozed, for when his head jerked upright in sudden shock, awake, the sun stood, red-tinted, on the rim of the horizon at the western windows of the house. The afternoon had gone. He sat for a time in the chair. A car came down the driveway and stopped at the front door. He stood up.

Mrs Sinclair, exiting from her daughter's red Volkswagen, managed with humour and an intuitive sense of mime to convey how totally unsuited these little foreign dodgem cars were to Californian living. Scrooging around in her seat, letting the door fly open, sliding her long legs out onto the tarmac, then, bunching her torso to avoid hitting her head against the roof, she emerged cautiously, rearing to her full height of six feet one inch alongside four feet eleven inches of Volkswagen. Dani, who had already opened the nose of the car, extracted her mother's overnight bag from it. Fergus, standing vacantly at the front door, stared at the bag, forgetting his manners, as he had forgotten they had invited her.

'Why, hello there,' Mrs Sinclair called, advancing on Fergus.

'Hello there, how are you?' Fergus said, his words becoming muffled as Mrs Sinclair folded her arms about him, pressing his face against her full breasts. Her red hair, in contrast to her daughter's, was cut very short, giving her the look of a large boy, a look abetted by her costume, which was a white, crew-neck, fisherman-knit sweater, worn with faded blue jeans. Her feet were bare.

'Well, nice to see you again,' she said.

'Nice to see you,' Fergus echoed. He looked at Dani, and under pretence of going over to carry Mrs Sinclair's bag, went to Dani, pushed aside her long red tresses, kissed the nape of her neck, and whispered in her ear that he was sorry.

'Sorry about what?'

Her mother was listening; he knew it. 'About this morning,' he mumbled.

'Oh that.' She laughed, and reaching up, kissed him affectionately, inexpertly, on the tip of his nose.

Fergus observed Mrs Sinclair observing, saw her watchful smile waver, then expand in relief. He took the overnight bag from Dani and smiled at her smiling mother, who at once spread her arms as though acknowledging applause. 'Why,' said Mrs Sinclair, 'this place is just, well, it's just too much. Yes, it really is something.'

Going on with it as they showed her inside. 'The sea and this beach and your lovely terrace, when I think of it, it's so perfect for a creative person. Dani told me it was peaceful, but, oh, why, it's just, oh, I wish *I* had a creative retreat like this.'

Dani opened a door. 'Mother, this will be your room.' But Mrs Sinclair did not enter. Instead, turning to Fergus, she took hold of his shoulder and shook him slightly, saying in an urgent voice, 'Now, it's not going to be like the other time we met, you're going to call me Dusty, do you hear me, now? Do you mind?'

'Not at all,' Fergus said.

'Oh, thank you. It means so much to me. I am a very lonely lady.' Mrs Sinclair leaned forward and kissed Fergus on the cheek, then smiled at her daughter. 'Why, he's just adorable.'

And, preceded by Dani, went into the room prepared for her. Fergus waited outside. All day, when the apparitions were not actually present, part of his mind had been wondering how he could explain them to Dani. And there was Boweri's visit; he must tell her about that. Alone. He had met Dani's mother only once before, over dinner in a restaurant in Santa Monica, and had felt uneasy about inviting her out here to stay overnight in a house where he shared the master bedroom with her daughter. But when he confessed these fears to Dani, she laughed and said she never heard of anything so square in her whole life, if only he knew her mother, if he *knew* Dusty, it was funny, it was hilarious, Dani said. Forget it.

So here was Dani's mother, Dusty, who would sleep in the room adjoining theirs tonight, and now Dani came out of her mother's room, warning him, by a headshake, not to whisper, instead, taking hold of his arm, walking him away up the corridor towards the kitchen, saying conversationally, 'Have a good day?'

'Fantastic.'

'Work went well, hmm?'

'No, no, I don't mean in a work sense. I mean something amazing happened. I must tell you about it.'

'Let me guess. They phoned? They love the script?'

'No, no, nothing like that. It had to do with the past. With my father and mother.'

She looked at him with momentary curiosity, shaking back her long tresses. 'Some insight?' she asked. *Her* mother was in group therapy; she was used to discussions of oedipal rage.

'No,' said Fergus. 'I know it sounds crazy, but they appeared to me. I mean right here in this house. And not only my parents. Other people too.'

'Ah-so,' said Dani in her Chinese impersonation, one which secretly depressed Fergus and made him wonder if he overestimated her intelligence. 'So now we make-um food appear. All light?'

He nodded. They went into the kitchen. 'Boweri was here.'

'You mean for real? Or just in your mind?'

'For real.'

'No kidding! So?'

He told her.

'And are you going to call him tonight?' she asked.

'You mean about the changes?'

'Mnn'hmm.'

'No.'

Dani laughed. 'You kill me. After all that worrying, you tell him to go stick it.'

'I did, didn't I?' Fergus said. 'What do you think? Was I right?'

'If you did it, you did it,' Dani said. 'Do your thing.' Discussions with her were, he found, frustrating. Her generation seemed to have no desire to worry the pros and cons of a situation.

'But what do *you* think?' he persisted.

'Ah, waddent know what to thenk,' Dani said in her Texas accent. 'You all, don't let nobody twist your arm, y'heah?'

'I won't get paid,' he said. 'I'll have to find some other job. I mean for the divorce and alimony and all that. It's going to delay things.'

'Then we won't have these Dear Abby sessions about marriage, first thing in the morning,' Dani said, smiling, sticking out her tongue at him. In the distance, he saw Mrs Sinclair hovering, solitary in the corridor, not knowing whether to interrupt.

'Darling, I'm sorry about this morning,' he said in a low voice. 'I really am.'

'That's okay,' Dani said. 'My fault. My lousy temper.' Then turned, casually, pretending to notice her mother. 'There you are, Mom. Come on in. Fergus, how about if you make us all a drink while I trim the steaks?'

'Fine,' he said. Mrs Sinclair, approaching up the corridor,

turned to peer through the windows, pantomiming pleasure. 'Why, looky there. A hummingbird! Cute!'

'What will you have to drink, Mrs Sinclair? I mean, Dusty.'

'Why, whatever you children are having.'

But as she entered the living room, Mrs Sinclair paused and mimed a reappraisal. 'No – oo, I think I'll change my mind and have a vodka martini, straight up. If you have vodka?'

'We do,' Fergus said. He went to the table where he kept the drinks.

'You said your parents appeared to you? Wasn't that what you just said?' Dani called from the kitchen. He did not answer. *Damn* her. 'Tell Mother. Mother went through the whole bit, séances and what have you. Remember Dr Gentleman, Mom?'

'That goddam crook,' Mrs Sinclair said. 'But Fergie, tell me, did you have a meeting with someone who's passed on?'

'I suppose so.'

'Do you often have psychic experiences?'

'Only on pot,' Dani called out.

'I do *not* smoke pot,' Fergus said, and realized he had imitated the righteous tone used by his father when correcting a falsehood.

'Well, I do,' Mrs Sinclair said, and giggled.

'Fergus is very uptight about pot and the drug scene,' Dani said. 'Mother, could you come and cut the ends off some asparagus, okay?'

'Why, surely.'

'Here you are,' Fergus said, handing Mrs Sinclair a vodka martini. 'And here's one for Dani. Will you excuse me a moment?'

'Certainly will.'

He watched Dani's mother go into the kitchen with the drinks, then turned and went into the guest bathroom, locking the door. He sat on the toilet seat. He felt slightly sick. His face, larger than life, stared at him from the magnified side of Dani's make-up mirror. Strange cratered eye sockets, pitted skin, eyes sad and lost and strange. Remembering the verdict of that afternoon: 'That man, wi' his teeth loose in his jaw, combing his hair over his bald spot, telling himself he's in love wi' a lassie who's young enough to be his daughter.'

His daughter? The first time he saw her, he was living in Western Motor Homes, and his neighbour, Dick Fowler, asked him over for a drink. When he arrived, there was Dick wearing a buckskin shirt, coloured neckscarf and moccasins, and with him this beautiful young girl, her long red hair bound at her temples by a squaw headband, and she wearing a short khaki tunic dress with no brassiere and it front-laced so loosely by leather thongs that Fergus had trouble keeping his eyes on her face. Hippies, he had thought, and kids, he had thought, and sad jealousy he had felt against Dick (unemployed, for godsakes!), who nevertheless had this lovely girl to go to bed with. Or had he thought even that clearly, so busy had he been trying to peek through her front-lacing without seeming to. Ugly, he had felt, and dull, and at first had no notion that she was paying any attention to him. After all, why should she look at him?

Sitting on the toilet seat, he bared his teeth in a grimace, the teeth enlarged in the magnifying mirror, remembering James Joyce's comment that in his forties he had a head filled with decaying ambitions and a mouth filled with rotting teeth. It comforted Fergus, that remark, but his dental problems were indubitably more severe than Joyce's caries. Fergus's gums were receding, leaving his teeth loose in his jaw. In the past few months his lower front teeth seemed to have become noticeably longer. *Long in the tooth*. Dani must notice those teeth, just as she must notice that little bald spot at the crown of his head, the part he combed hair over so carefully, but to what purpose, since the minute he got into bed with her it became disarranged, showing that it was not just thin, he was going bald, yes, a man in his late thirties with a bald spot and loose teeth (drifting, the dentist had said) in his jaws; in fact, he had given up going to the dentist since the dentist had advised him that crowns or even bridges would not arrest the damage, better settle for extractions and a full denture, the dentist said. Fergus shut his mouth on his loose, magnified teeth and turned Dani's mirror around, hoping that on the other side, in the smaller projection, his face would seem better-looking. But in the smaller projection his face, no longer blurred by magnification, was lined, harder, the face of an ageing young man under a false winter tan.

Yet it was *his* face. He smiled at it, trying to cheer it up, that face which had stared at the living-room wall this afternoon, hearing all its irrational fears, self-accusations, and doubts voiced by the enemies it knew were somewhere, speaking out against it, a face of no conviction, its smile failing, not sure if those accusations were true or false, or partly both. 'Isn't there an answer?' his younger persona had pleaded. But the kangaroo court dissolved as soon as the issue was posed. As Maeve had disappeared earlier in the day when he asked a similar question. Why was this happening? What was it he must find out? But his mirror face could not tell him: it was graven as a face on a coin.

'Fergus? Fergus?' That was Dani calling.

'Yes?'

'Want to do the steaks on the hibachi?'

Dani is here in the house; her mother is here. There have been no apparitions for more than an hour. He stood up and unlocked the bathroom door. Dani was standing outside, her drink in her hand. 'Okay, sweet?' she said. 'Are you all right?'

He nodded. What can she see in me? Will she get tired of me?

'You sure? You look sort of funny?'

'I'm fine,' he said. 'Do you like me?'

She grinned at him. 'Of course I like you, you nut. Now, put the coals on, will you?'

Crimson, mauve, violet, orange, black, the mixture as before, each evening slightly different in its vulgar palette, but recognizably the same Pacific picture-postcard sunset, exotic, warm, beautiful, exactly the kind of sunset to be watching, as, slightly high, one squatted on the terrace of a rented beach house in California, turning prime steaks on a discount-store hibachi grill. With Mrs Dusty Sinclair and her daughter – how was it, it went? He remembered and, tunelessly, sang it out:

> 'Oh, the moon shines bright on Mrs Porter,
> And on her daughter
> They wash their feet in soda water.'

'Is that an English song?' Mrs Sinclair asked, as, carefully balancing her third martini, she swung in the egg chair, smiling at the sunset.

'No, it's from a poem.'

'You've got to be kidding?'

'It's *The Waste Land*. T. S. Eliot.'

'You're kidding me?'

'Poetry is Fergus's *shtick*,' Dani said. 'He wouldn't kid you about that.'

Fergus blew on the charcoal briquettes, reflecting that Dani had picked up the word *shtick* from him, as he had picked it up from Redshields, and that he was now sick of *shtick*. He also noticed that Dani's mother was able to touch the ground with her feet while sitting in the egg chair. She was at home in the egg chair. His father was not.

'There's a guy in Malibu made something like a half a million bucks from his poems,' Mrs Sinclair said. 'He used to be a disc jockey. I saw him on "The Johnny Carson Show." He's real cute.'

'Oh, Mother!'

'Well, he *is* cute,' Mrs Sinclair said defensively. 'You know something, Ferg? I embarrass my daughter. I mean, not everybody can be superfragiliferous intelligent, right?'

'Oh, Mother! Fergus doesn't want to hear all that!'

'All what? That you're ashamed of me, that you're worried Fergus will think you're dumb because you think *I'm* dumb, right?'

Dani, who had been mixing salad in a large salad bowl, put down the wooden mixing spoons. 'Okay,' she said. She turned and went over to the egg chair. 'Come on, Mom. Come inside, I want to talk to you.'

Mrs Sinclair, looking at first angry, then confused, allowed herself to be extracted from the egg chair, and still holding her martini glass, went with Dani into the house. The glass doors were pulled shut. Fergus, watching, imagined himself in Mrs Sinclair's place. It was, he thought, just how Dani would act if, suddenly, she decided to end it with him. Abrupt, decisive, no quarter. He put down the barbecue fork and looked sombrely at the steaks. He stood, stretching his legs, and as he did, realized that he was not alone.

Peggy Sanford sat on a white garden chair at the far end of the terrace. She was watching him. She was small – a slip of a girl, her mother had called her. She wore the yellow, high-busted silk dress she had worn on Capri the night they were driven out from their room in the Quisisana Hotel by omnipresent, persistent mosquitoes. Her lipstick was bright red, almost black now under the beam of the yellow terrace lamp. She was smoking, as always, and with a small emotive pain he noticed her right hand, the middle finger with its top two joints cut off, the stump, capped by skin, nailless. She was abnormally sensitive about that finger, and when she met strangers would clench her fist, avoiding a handshake.

She was that person he did not speak of, the one he hoped never to meet again. When he left Europe for America he was twenty-four years old. She kissed him good-bye at the Aerogare de Paris. In a year he was to send for her: they were to be married. He thought of the only conversation they had had since – her excited voice, eight months later, on the transatlantic telephone telling him she had booked a charter flight and would be arriving in New York for a two-week holiday. When she phoned, he had not thought of her in weeks, and was, in fact, living with a girl in Greenwich Village. Confused, he had told her the truth. He said he was sorry. 'Don't be,' she said. 'It's all right. Good-bye, Fergus.' She hung up. He never heard from her again. Someone told him she had married a French surgeon (a Communist) and was living in Lausanne. Someone else said she had been married but was now divorced and back in Paris, working as an interpreter for UNESCO. She was that person he had betrayed. He found it painful to look at her.

But she did not sound angry. 'Fergus,' she said, 'I'll bet I know why you thought of me.'

'Why?'

'Seeing that old Yankee one drunk. She reminds you of my Mam, doesn't she?'

'She's not *really* like her,' Fergus said, and they both laughed. Peggy's mother was a Scot, a waitress in a fish-and-chips café in the Finchley Road in London. The first morning that Fergus ever woke up in bed with Peggy, in Peggy's dingy top-floor flat in a house in Belsize Road, there was a knock on the bedroom door, and, dressed as a waitress, in apron, cap, and black frock, a strange drunk woman walked in and laid a tray of bacon, eggs, toast, and tea on the bedspread.

'This is my Mam,' Peggy told him. Her Mam grinned. 'Have you no pants on?' her Mam asked Fergus. He blushed. 'Well, watch yourself then, getting out of bed,' said Peggy's drunk Mam. 'There's an old one across the way that has opera glasses. She's wanting to call the police and have us chucked out of here. You'll excuse the uniform,' said Peggy's drunk Mam, 'but I'm on the early turn down at the caff.'

Now, remembering, Fergus smiled at Peggy, sitting on the white garden chair in her good silk dress, looking out at the Pacific Ocean as she had once, on their Italian holiday together, looked out at the clear water of the Mediterranean from the Marina Piccola in Capri. 'How *is* your Mam?' he asked.

'She's grand. She got married again.'

'How many's that?'

'Five,' said Peggy. There was a pause.

'I heard *you* got married,' he said.

'I heard *you* did,' she said.

'A mistake. I'm trying to get a divorce.'

'Are you?' said Peggy. 'You've weathered well, do you know that, Fergus? I thought you'd look much older.'

'You were always charitable,' Fergus said. 'It's amazing how clearly I remember you after all these years.'

'But *do* you remember me, Fergus? Do you really?'

'Do you remember Capri?' he asked. 'The two of us under that sheet, waiting for the mosquitoes to come back? And the bites!'

'And getting dressed at five and going out to see the sun come up on the Ferraglioni rocks,' Peggy said.

'And the next day we had a big fight about Murray Price. You ran out of that Axel Munthe house in a temper because I said something about Murray's Lenin beard.'

Peggy laughed. 'He didn't like you, either, old Murray. What was it he said one time about you – oh, yes, he said that your bourgeois background made you indifferent to the historical imperatives of the working class.'

They both laughed. 'Sounds like him.' Fergus said. 'Stupid clot! What the hell did *he* ever do for the working class?'

'Ah, well,' said Peggy 'You have to give him that. He *tried*. Remember he had his jaw broken by the police in Stockholm? His face has never been the same since.'

'It wasn't my favourite face to begin with,' Fergus said. 'Your Communist Casanova.'

'Don't make fun. Poor Murray, I told you that stuff about him in confidence. I heard later on you made a funny story out of it. That was hurtful, Fergus. To him, *and* to me.'

'Who said I said that?' Fergus blustered, but, guilty, remembered he had joked about Murray and Peggy. There were some people you behaved badly towards. Peggy was one of those people. And then, guilty, Fergus remembered something *she* might feel guilty about. Georges de Foresta told him four years ago not to feel badly about having deserted Peggy. Georges said a month after Fergus left for America, Peggy was in the Mabilleon every night with a new boyfriend. An Italian political-science student, Georges said. They lived together in Peggy's apartment, Georges said.

He looked at Peggy. There was one thing about her. If you asked her whether or not she had slept with some Italian student, she would tell you the truth. She was a great one for the truth. But how could he ask, after what he had done to her?

The glass doors slid open behind him. Dani came out onto the terrace. Precipitately, he went to the forgotten hibachi and turned the steaks over. Dani came to the grill and hunkered down beside him, whispering, 'Okay now, but, listen, don't give Mom any more to drink. She gets kind of mean sometimes.'

Alarmed, he turned to look at the garden chair. Peggy had vanished. Relief merged with a sense of disappointment about his unasked question. At that moment, Mrs Sinclair reappeared on the terrace. 'My,' said she, 'do those steaks ever smell good!'

'They're overdone, I'm afraid.'

'Let's eat,' Dani said.

Mrs Sinclair had once worked in films. At the age of fifty-four she was trying to break into television. 'The average person would be discouraged,' she told Fergus. 'But not me. I'd be discouraged only if I quit. You know what I mean, Ferg? "Joshua fit de battle ob Jericho and de walls came tumblin' down." Dani will tell you what I've gone through, eh, doll?'

Dani, helping Fergus to ice-cream pie, smiled the embarrassed smile of a child whose parent has insisted it recite. 'Long as I can remember,' Dani said, 'it's been a new agent, a new contract, some casting director she's heard of, and there she is, doing the rounds every day she's not working. Never stops.'

'You have a regular job, then?' Fergus asked.

Mrs Sinclair grinned and ruffled her short hair as though she were about to wash it. 'See this? Know why I keep it like this? Because I work in a beauty parlour, that's why. Women getting their hair done, it makes me sick to my stomach. I mean, if I thought that's the way I was going to end my days, like some of the women I see in this place I work, well, I tell you, I'd give up right now. God, it's depressing, getting old. I envy you, you writers, it doesn't matter what you look like, your creativity goes on. I used to see a lot of writers in the old days when I was under contract to Metro –'

'Come on, Ma, you never were under contract to Metro,' Dani interrupted.

'I was. In forty-six, I was.'

'You were not.'

'What do you know?' Mrs Sinclair asked. 'You weren't even born.' She turned to Fergus. 'Kids these days, they're full of crap, they walk all over you.'

Fergus tried a non-committal smile, but failed, for, a little to the left of Mrs Sinclair, his own mother, dressed in mourning black, was shaking her head at Aunt Kate (Mother Mary Gonzaga), semaphoring with her eyebrows that Reverend Mother should listen to this. Aunt Kate, whose pious, hairy face reminded Fergus of the Gilbert Stuart portrait of George Washington, wore the white guimpe and black headdress of the Order of the Sisters of Mercy, and now, as she peered around her headdress in the harnessed manner of nuns, the movement was so vivid in his memory that, set against the clarity of it, Dani and Mrs Sinclair seemed improbable characters in a wide-screen colour film of American life. Reverend Mother and his own mother, hallucinations though they might be, moved in this room with a presence stronger than that of the living women – Dani and Mrs Sinclair – he had known as an adult. His mother and Aunt Kate he had seen, smelled, and sensed with the special strong perceptions of a very young child. And so, as the apparitions moved closer, confident, as though this were their own house, Fergus looked at Dani. But if Dani saw Mrs Fadden and Reverend Mother, she gave no sign. Certainly, Mrs Sinclair, who sat with her back to them, had noticed nothing unusual, for now, leaning towards Fergus, she gripped his thigh under the table, and kneading it, said urgently, '*You* believe me, don't you?'

'What?' said Fergus. They are becoming bolder, he thought. What if they begin to speak to me, even when other people are here in the room?

'About Fox. I was under contract to Fox.'

'You told us it was Metro you were under contract to,' Dani said, laughing. 'Metro, you said!'

'Did I? Well, I worked for all the majors, one time or another. You'd never believe it to look at me now, Ferg, but one thing I was, and that was beautiful. Beautiful!'

His mother and Reverend Mother had their heads together, whispering. What shocked them, as it shocked him, was Mrs Sinclair's hand, under the table, caressing his thigh. Reverend Mother, her breath hissing in scandalized intake, joined her hands together gothically, and at once began what must be a silent prayer for the salvation of Fergus's immortal soul. His own mother looked as though she might, at any moment, do Mrs Sinclair some bodily harm.

'The trouble is,' Mrs Sinclair told Fergus, 'a person can't stand still. I mean, now it's a whole new bag for me. For the last ten years, well, maybe even more than ten, I've had to go for character roles. You can't be an ingenue at forty. You can try to be a swinger, though.'

'A swinger?' said Fergus's mother. 'What does she mean, Kate?'

Reverend Mother made the Sign of the Cross, finishing her prayer. 'Come along, Julia,' said Reverend Mother. 'This is no place for the likes of you and me.'

'I mean I'm not ready to play Victoria Regeena,' Mrs Sinclair said. 'And I never was the Doris Day type, you know. I've told my new agent he should think of me for a Lucille Ball situation. Attractive older woman, maybe in a comedy segment.'

'Come, Julia!' whispered Reverend Mother, looking very much like an unattractive older woman in a comedy segment.

'Lucille Ball,' Fergus's mother said. 'I remember her, she's an American one, she was in the pictures.'

'Come along,' Reverend Mother said. '*Please*, Julia?'

Fergus smiled at Mrs Sinclair. Behind him, as she moved towards the doors, he heard the impatient rustle of Reverend Mother's black serge habit and the jingle of the large black rosary beads, knotted in the belt at her waist.

'I mean, it doesn't have to be comedy,' Mrs Sinclair said, taking his smile for scepticism. 'Would you buy an older woman, period? Maybe you have something you're writing? There might be such a part, hmm?'

'Oh, Mother!' Dani said.

'Julia!' said Reverend Mother. 'I will count to three. If you don't come then, I will leave this room on my own!'

'Dani, Fergus is in the *business!*' Mrs Sinclair said. 'How often do I get to talk to anyone in the business, these days?'

Fergus, watching his mother's face, saw that she had not understood. *What* business? her confused look clearly asked. He answered his mother's unspoken question. 'I'm in show business,' he said, 'I guess.'

'Well, *aren't* you?' Mrs Sinclair asked. 'I mean, I understood you were writing a screenplay?'

'Yes, I was.'

Fergus's mother turned and looked significantly at Reverend

Mother. To his surprise and irritation, her look was one of boastful pride. 'Did you hear that, Kate? He's writing a film!'

'A comedy, is it?' Mrs Sinclair asked.

'It's a novel I wrote.'

'One!' said Reverend Mother. 'Two!' said Reverend Mother.

'Well,' said Mrs Sinclair, 'shoot me for trying, but if you have any part, even a small part? Look, I'd settle for a walk-on. It would be an honour to be associated with something you've written.'

'Mother, please!' Dani said.

'Ferg doesn't mind my asking, do you, Ferg? He can only say no. Right, Ferg?'

'Three!' said Reverend Mother.

'Oh, please, Kate,' Fergus's mother pleaded. 'Just one second?'

'Good night, Julia,' said Reverend Mother. Her habit rustling, her sensible shoes loud on the bricks, she went out of the opened glass doors onto the moonlit terrace. Where do they go when they walk away like that? Fergus wondered. Perhaps to the children's playhouse, the one in the abandoned playground behind the bougainvillea bush? Fergus's mother lingered, guiltily; a nun is not supposed to go out by herself at night, and Reverend Mother had been forced to go alone.

'Because, listen to me,' Mrs Sinclair told Fergus. 'If I give up now, I'm going to wind up a lonely old lady. And goddammit, I don't want that to happen. That's why I've got to keep on trying, right?'

'Mother, everybody has troubles,' Dani said. 'Fergus has problems of his own.'

'I know,' Mrs Sinclair said, gripping Fergus's hand in her own. 'That wife of yours! Wow, Dani told me!'

At mention of the word 'wife' Fergus's mother frowned in disapproval and, frowning, made her exit, following Reverend Mother out to the terrace.

'I meant work problems,' Dani said.

'Oh?' Mrs Sinclair removed her hand from Fergus's hand. 'But you make a good living, don't you? I mean, being a book author and all?'

'Mother,' Dani said, 'come on, let's clear up.'

Mrs Sinclair, winking to show Fergus she would much rather stay and talk, followed Dani down the long room, past the opened glass doors, going into the kitchen, which adjoined the living room and which also opened on the brick-tiled terrace facing the sea. There, Dani and her mother with easy, efficient Californian movements began to load the electric dishwasher, dispose of waste through the electric garburator, and prepare coffee in the electric grinder. In the combined noise of these appliances, conversation was impossible, so the women, working, no longer looked at each other or tried to converse with Fergus, who, sitting alone at the dining table, looked at the moonlit terrace wondering if his mother and Aunt Kate were walking out there, scandalized, discussing his present life. The moonlight was stark and eerie. The egg chairs swung in the silver light, and below the terrace, on the beach, waves flipped over, like the pages of a book, their long crests lit by a strip of phosphorescence in the instant before they flattened and fell on the sands. He rose and walked towards the terrace doors, but as he did, Dani, arranging coffee cups on a tray, signalled that she wanted to speak to him. Uneasy, as though he had planned to deceive her, he waited, smiling uncomfortably as she came towards him and drew him out onto the terrace. He looked about in the moonlight. No one.

'I'm sorry,' Dani said.

'What about?'

'Mother.'

'Nonsense. She's okay.'

'Not for me. She drives me nuts. God, it's awful to despise your own mother.'

'Go on,' he said. 'You're very fond of her.'

'No, I love her but I don't like her. She makes me ashamed. Coming on to you like that about her, quote, career, unquote.'

He laughed.

'Then, afterwards, I hate myself for despising her,' Dani said. 'What right have I to despise her? I know what it is. I'm afraid, maybe, in some way I'm like her.'

'*You* – like her?' He shook his head. He realized that Dani was close to tears. He had never seen her cry before, and so, touched by these imminent tears, took her in his arms, hugged her, and said, 'You're not in the least like her. You never worked for the majors.'

Which made her laugh and break away from him. 'I mustn't stay out here. She'll think we're plotting against her. She's a bit paranoid, poor Ma.'

'Okay. Let's go in.'

'No. Wait. I'll help her finish the dishes. You come in, in a minute.'

She smiled at him, wiped the corners of her eyes, and went into the house. In the moonlight, all was blacks and whites; cold, unreal, strange. He thought of Dani's surprising tears and looked in at the kitchen, where mother and daughter stood, busy at the efficient sinks, handsome, red-haired women, personification of the American way. Affectionate, almost sisterly in their bright play clothes. Yet Dusty can make Dani weep, Dani who never weeps. Why? Because parents form the grammar of our emotions. As mine have mine, Fergus thought, turning away from this pretty picture, this world so different from the old worlds he had known; walking down the terrace, past the bougainvillea bushes, his feet rustling among the dried bougainvillea blossoms scattered on the ground, blossoms which in daylight were a faded orange, but now were silver and black, the false blooms of some lunar landscape. In the little playground, screened by the bougainvillea bush, there was a child's gym set with two swings, climbing ladder, and a hobbyhorse, all left unpainted by a former tenant when the child for whom these things were built died in its mother's womb. Unused, neglected in the overgrowth of grass and weeds, the swings and hobbyhorse reminded Fergus simultaneously of a primitive jungle painting by Henri Rousseau and of a turn-of-the-century playground he used to pass by every day in the Luxembourg Gardens, a playground on whose old-fashioned swings and hobbyhorses he imagined the boy Marcel Proust might have played. Now he moved past the swings, walking under the bedraggled plumes of a tall eucalyptus tree, and to the left of a stunted Torrey pine, came on the Hansel and Gretel playhouse, its roof ten feet high at the apex, tilted slightly, as after a storm. He stooped and went in at the doorway, then, straightening to his full height inside, saw, in the light of the solitary playhouse windows, two rows of wooden benches, and at the end of the room, a toy stove on top of which were toy plastic teacups and a teapot. He sat, tentatively, on one of the benches. Was this where the apparitions went when they walked out of sight past the bougainvillea bushes? Was this haunted ground? Sensing a fear he had last known as a schoolboy when he ventured at night into the moonlit battlements of Doe Castle in Donegal. There, in the grass- and weed-filled courtyard amid the smell of cow dung, he had looked up at the ruined keep from which men had been flung to their deaths in the bloody days of MacSweeney NadTuath. And, as he stood in the death-haunted yard, rain came, eerie in the moonlight, a sudden silent chastisement of rain; but he did not move; he feared the dark shelter of the ruined eaves. Soaked by the downpour, his skin prickling, sure that he was being watched, sure that the ghost of MacSweeney would strike him dead for having ventured into his domain, he fell to his knees, in panic, reciting an act of contrition, believing it his last end.

And now? Was an act of contrition from him what these apparitions sought?

Someone coughed. Fergus looked up. At the little window of the playhouse, framed in the window as in a confessional grille, his head bowed, Father Vincent Byrne, parish priest of the Church of the Most Holy Redeemer, Belfast.

Father Byrne nodded his head, indicating that he was ready to start. 'How long since your last confession?' he asked, putting the routine opening question, waiting, confident of a quick answer.

How long? Confused, Fergus tried to think back. 'Well, it must be about – twenty-five years.'

'Twenty-five years,' the priest said non-committally.

'No, wait, I'm sure it must be longer, I mean, since I made an honest confession. The confessions I made in my teens, I didn't tell the whole truth. That was my trouble. I kept things back.'

'Ergo, you made a bad confession,' Father Byrne said. 'Ergo, you committed a mortal sin and a sacrilege. Did you go to Holy Communion during this period of mortal sin?'

'Yes.'

'That is a very grave sacrilege. How long is it, then, since you have been in the state of grace?'

'I never, I mean, I don't think I ever was in the state of grace.'

'This is not so, my child,' the priest said. 'Remember your first confession and your first communion, when you were just a little boy? At that time, of course, you were in a state of grace.'

'But that's what I'm trying to tell you. From the very beginning I had some sort of doubt. I don't think I ever really believed.'

'Not true,' the priest said. 'You were afraid; therefore, you believed.'

'I suppose that's right,' Fergus said. 'But that was the extent of my faith. A boy's fear of hell and damnation. Not very much of a credit to your teachings, is it? The limits of a child's fear.'

'There are no limits to a child's fear,' the priest said. 'Therefore you have been in a state of mortal sin for more than thirty years.'

On a nearby bluff, a neighbour's dog barked, as though sensing an intruder in the night. Fergus moved his foot on the wooden floor of the playhouse. His foot made a scraping noise.

'Sin,' the priest said, 'is of two kinds. Sins of omission and sins of commission. Let us begin with the sins of omission, with the things you have neglected to do.'

'Well, I know I haven't worked as hard, writing, I mean. I've wasted time, taken holidays, journalism, hangovers, hack work, the lot. I mean, I know I might have done more –'

'Yes, of course, of course,' the priest said in an irritated voice. 'We must all use the capabilities God gave us to the best of our abilities. But not for ambition's sake. No. For the greater glory of God. Now, that, it seems, is your failing, my child. Your concerns are temporal. And you know the saying: "What doth it profit a man if he gain the whole world and suffer the loss of his immortal soul?"'

'But just because I don't believe in an afterlife,' Fergus said, 'that doesn't mean my ambition is a simple matter of wish for personal gain. It's, rather, a feeling that we have only one life. It's the Calvinistic conscience, or whatever you want to call it; a desire to achieve some worthwhile goal.'

'What goal?' said the priest. 'It is not, so far as I can see, even the normal agnostic goal of helping one's fellow man for the sake of humanity. No, no, a literary goal is what you are talking about. What you feel guilty about is that you haven't done more to further your prideful ambitions. What about the things you *should* feel guilty about? The ten commandments, the seven deadly sins. It seems you have committed most of those.'

'Here we go, sex, sex, sex!' Fergus said, irritated. 'I'm not talking about that.'

' *Your* great sin,' said the priest, 'is the sin against the Holy Ghost. It is a six-part sin, of which the first part is presumption, the second is despair, the third is resisting the known truth, the fourth is envy of others' spiritual goodness, the fifth is obstinacy in sin, and the sixth and last is final impenitence. You had forgotten that sin, eh, Fadden?'

'Hardly,' said Fergus. 'Since I've remembered it now.' He looked up, pleased that he had made this point. But the window was empty. There were, he decided, rules governing these appearances. The moment he had realized it was he and not Father Byrne who had detailed the six-part sin against the Holy Ghost, the spell had been broken. When he had ceased to believe in Father Byrne, Father Byrne had ceased to be.

'Sloppy, woolly thinking!' A sharp pain in the lobe of his ear caused Fergus to jerk sideways. Tugging on the ear was the Very Reverend Daniel Keogh, M.A., D.D., president of St Michan's College for Boys, Belfast. 'Up, sir, UP!' cried Dr Keogh, dragging Fergus to his feet. In his left hand Dr Keogh held a long rattan cane with which, cruelly, he began to flog Fergus about the shanks. 'Aha! So that's how we reason, is it? So poor Father Byrne does not exist because you, sir, do not believe he exists. Hah! And I suppose Almighty God does not exist simply because the miserable imagination of Fergus Fadden isn't capable of conceiving of His existence? Right hand, right hand! Out with the flipper!'

The cane nudged Fergus's right arm, commanding him to raise it up, which he did, extending it fully as he had been taught to do, his palm out, flat, waiting for the blow. Dr Keogh sighted, raised the cane over his head, and brought it down with whistling force. But, at the last second, Fergus pulled his hand away, partly from fear, partly because he realized where he was. The cane, un-impeded by his palm, smacked loudly against the thick black skirt of the headmaster's soutane.

'Pull away, would you? Hah! That will cost you dear!' Dr Keogh cried. 'Double the dose, double the dose! Out with that flipper! Hup there!'

And stood, avenger, cane over his head, grey hair curling in long wisps around his ears, eyes fiery, mouth pulled down in rage like a Japanese funerary mask. 'Well, sir,' Dr Keogh yelled. 'Come along, sir!'

It couldn't be happening, the priest couldn't be going to beat him, he was not a boy, he was a grown man –

'Father!' he cried. 'Look at me, I'm grown up, I'm a parent, I'm an American citizen –'

Whish! Dr Keogh brought the cane down. It hit Fergus on the shoulder blade. It cut into his skin. Fergus cried out in pain, and lunging forward, seized hold of Dr Keogh, his fingers closing on the black stuff of the old priest's soutane, just below the waxy clerical collar. He pulled the old priest towards him, wrenched the cane from his hand, and releasing the old man, tried to break the cane in two over his knee. But, strong and pliant, the cane would not break. The old priest, panting, shook his head as though watching some poor lunatic, whereupon Fergus, incensed, shot out his right hand, caught the priest once more by the collar, and with his left hand, began to slap the old man's face, left, right, right, left, as hard as he could hit; and as he hit, hit, hit, he heard his own voice moaning, 'Ahhhhhh – Ahhhhhhh – Ahhhhhh!' Hitting, hitting, hitting at that which he had wanted to hit all his life. Panting, he tried to catch his breath, paused, then, remembering the cane, let go of the old priest, and scrabbling on the playhouse floor, found the cane and rose up with it, an awful, triumphant smile on his face. 'What about *this?*' he yelled. 'Double the dose, eh, double the dose!' And raised the cane over his head, bringing it down on the old man's shoulders, beating, beating, revenging himself and all other boys.

The old priest, whimpering, protecting his neck and head, cried out, 'Ah no, please, sir, no . . .'

It was the cry Fergus had heard a school boarder utter once

when Dr Keogh beat him for smoking in the jakes, a cry of terror, pleading, hopeless, and now, hearing the old man repeat that cry, Fergus threw aside the cane and sat, slumped on the child's bench, beginning to weep, weeping, holding his head in his hands until the weeping wore itself out and he was alone in the playhouse, weak, like someone wakened from a nightmare; but it was no normal nightmare, his hands still stung, he could remember the feel of the cloth of the old man's soutane, the bristles on the old man's ill-shaven cheek, the pliant rattan cane, and he knew that he had hit and hit; and I am just like they were, he thought, I am no different. I stood there yelling with pleasure as I beat him. I could have killed him.

And there, in the child's playhouse, he put his head between his knees as though warding off a faint. *I could have killed him.* But Dr Keogh is dead. As my father and mother are dead, as Maeve is no longer sixteen and Peggy Sanford no longer twenty-three. Perhaps that is why these people are able to appear to me in California? Because they no longer exist as such on earth. The past has come back to crowd out my present.

'Fergus?'

Dani; he heard her on the terrace, calling softly, worried. 'Fergus?'

Better not let her see he had been weeping. How could you explain what had happened with Dr Keogh without seeming like some mad sadist yourself? No matter how often he told her, there was no way she could really understand. She had never gone through a childhood like his.

'Fergus? Are you there?'

He sat quiet. Not yet. Perhaps only the past is real. The past cannot change, whereas anyone I know now is capable of becoming an entirely different person when next they walk into my life.

Different, as though confirming his thought, Dani appeared outside the playhouse, searching for him over by the bougain-villea bushes. Seen through the playhouse window, she seemed, not the girl who had been close to tears half an hour ago, but a stranger; there was something very childish about her, seen through the window – her very short dress, her long straight hair, her white plastic Wellington boots which came up to her knees.

Something ineluctably sexually titillating. She looked far younger than her years, so young that if he touched her he might be arrested for contributing to the delinquency of a minor. This sinful idea excited him, as it had in the past, making him tremble, making him wonder if he really was abnormal, for there was no fear, no joy, no sorrow, no serious thought he had ever entertained which could not, momentarily, be deflected by the sight of a pretty girl. He stood up. He felt better, much better. He stepped out of the playhouse.

'Hi,' he said.

She turned, saw him. 'What were you doing in there?'

'Going to confession.'

'You crazy nut!' she said, and laughed.

'How's your mother?'

'Oh, it's better. We kind of made up. Are you okay?'

She came close, looking into his eyes, worried for him. He put his hands on her shoulders and kissed her forehead, chastely, imagining himself as her evil guardian and she his innocent ward. Slipping his hands down to caress her breasts and thighs, his fingers searching to find the hem of her very short skirt, which he raised at the rear as she stood, submissive, quiet as a young animal in the moonlight, while he, her master, felt for and fondled the twin globes of her bottom. Stiff, he pressed against her, and then, his frightening encounter with Dr Keogh quite exorcised by this gratifying moment, he let her skirt fall, stepped back two paces, and went down on his knees before her.

'What are you doing?'

'Shh!' he said. 'Lift your skirt.'

She smiled. Unlike those girls he had known when *he* was her age, she understood what it was like suddenly to feel horny. Obedient, she raised her skirt, revealing her taut little tummy and the drawn V of her skimpy underpants. As a boy on his way to school in Belfast, he used to pass through a Protestant working-class district, row on curving row of small red-brick two-storey dwellings, no house different from its neighbours, except in its curtains or the ornaments in the front-parlour windows, ornaments which were turned towards the street for the edification of passers-by. A favourite piece of statuary seen in these parlour windows was a coloured pottery shepherdess, smiling as she held her skirts out to curtsy, revealing her drawers. He smiled at Dani, standing by the playhouse in the moonlight, holding up her skirt. Then he, her evil master, reached out both hands, pulled down the shepherdess's drawers, and smiling, buried his face in her soft bush.

Tickled by his touch, she shuddered and laughed.

'Dani? Dani?' (Her mother's voice).

'Damn,' said Dani, laying her hands on his head like a blessing as he kissed her between her legs. 'Come on, Fergus, get up.'

Fergus allowed her to move away; then, somewhat awkwardly, he felt, he got to his feet.

'Shh!' Dani said and pointed past the bougainvillea bushes. Mrs Sinclair stood on the terrace in the moonlight. 'Dani?' she called, then, looking about her, went back into the living room.

'Watch this!' Dani cautioned Fergus, going to him, taking him by the hand and leading him over to the bushes to spy on her mother. Inside the living room, Mrs Sinclair peered about her, then, surreptitiously, went towards the table which contained the drinks. Swiftly, she drank a large swallow straight from the gin bottle, then, refilling her glass, moved across the living room to sit on the yellow sofa, propping her bare feet up on the coffee table as though she had relaxed in that position for hours. Dani laughed lightly. 'There we go,' she said. 'And I was worried about her seeing *us*.'

The image of Mrs Sinclair finding him kneeling in the moonlight, his face buried between her daughter's legs, suddenly brought back Peggy Sanford's mother, marching in, dressed as a waitress, to serve him breakfast in bed, which in turn, made him think of his own parents, perhaps watching him from behind the bougainvillea bushes as he knelt in homage to Dani, his mother averting her eyes, her face hot, his father furious, scandalized. And as Fergus thought of this, he felt himself blush.

'Let's go in, baby,' Dani said, putting her arm around his waist as they moved towards the glass doors. She protected him. He would be all right. Soon he would go to bed with her and would sleep, and tomorrow all this would be remembered only as some sort of dream. At the doorway he stopped and kissed her. 'Don't ever leave me. Promise?'

She laughed. 'I pledge the oath of allegiance. Now, come on. Let's go in.'

'I'm serious.'

She laughed. 'Don't you think I am?'

'I don't know.'

'You nut!' she said, and kissed him. Perfunctorily, he thought. But he was grateful.

Lapped around by drinks, feet on the big coffee table, they watched a talk show on the portable television set. At least, Mrs Sinclair watched it; Dani divided her attention between the programme and her magazine, while Fergus watched Dani, his mind drifting back to the night he met her. Remembering how unreal Los Angeles seemed that first month. When he first arrived, he had phoned Dick Fowler for advice on where to stay. Dick and he had been friends in Greenwich Village. They had kept in touch. In New York, Dick had played young doctors on television soap operas, a style he aped in private life, affecting Brooks Brothers clothing and a precise diction. But in his native city of Los Angeles, Dick was a different person. He suggested that Fergus move into an efficiency apartment in a West Los Angeles motor court. Dick lived there himself, and 'it's cool,' the new Dick announced. 'It's near the action, and a groovy place to pick up chicks.' '*What* chicks?' Fergus wondered aloud to Dick, after he had lived in the place a month. In all that time the only people he had met in Los Angeles besides Dick were Boweri and Redshields and their wives. Dick said, 'But I didn't think you really wanted chicks, man, I thought you were creating.' Then suggested that Fergus come over to his place that evening for some margaritas and afterwards they would go out and look over the girl action on Sunset Strip. Dick's efficiency apartment was a twin to Fergus's in the same block of the motor court. That was the evening Fergus arrived to find Dick dressed in his new style, buckskin shirt, Apache scarf, and moccasins, and with him, Dani

Sinclair, her khaki tunic dress disturbingly front-laced with loose leather thongs, Dick's girl, Fergus assumed, seeing himself as odd man out for this evening on the town. She asked if he were writing a book about Los Angeles and Fergus, making conversation, said he wasn't, but if he were, he'd begin the book with a detailed description of the furniture in his two-room efficiency apartment. Like the French anti-novelists, he said, who write page after page describing furniture and ignoring people. 'Is that right?' Dick Fowler asked, and the girl said: 'Oh, yes, I remember. I read one by Robbe-Grillet.' And because she knew that and was beautiful, Fergus began to think her brilliant, and so explained his fancy, which was that Los Angeles was an interesting location for an anti-novel because it was post-capitalist and post-possessions. 'Take this place of Dick's, for example,' Fergus said. 'It's exactly the same as my place, four doors up. There are twenty apartments in this motor court, all exactly alike. Take this carpet. It looks like real wool, but it's made of nylon thread. The pile is burn-proof. Those two reading chairs have polished wooden frames and maroon tweed cushions. But the wood is synthetic, and so is the tweed. The chairs do not stain or burn. The table tops, cupboard doors, and other kitchen and dining surfaces are made of formica. Stains wash off. There is one picture in each apartment. The same picture. It appears to be an oil painting. But if you look on the back' – he turned the picture over and showed the girl and Dick the label:

REALOIL
Simulates the look and texture
of the original oil painting:
SUNFLOWERS
By Artist Vincent Van Gogh

'You see,' he told Dick and the girl, 'everything in these apartments is made of some type of synthetic material, which, if possible, is designed to look like the natural material it replaces. And these materials repel wear and tear. Stains wash off. I could live here for a year and leave no mark on anything. My presence would count for nothing. Last week I burned a hole in the green rayon spread which covers my bed. The Mexican maid they send in to clean saw the burn, took the spread away, and the same day there was a new spread, same colour, on the bed. No one mentioned the damage. I wasn't even charged for the burned bedspread.'

'Yes, but what are you getting at?' Dick Fowler asked.

So he had tried to explain to Dick and to this girl, Dani, the strange buried feeling he had, living in Los Angeles. 'It's as though everything here is designed to deny one's existence,' he said. 'For instance, do you know who owns this motor court?' Dick said, no he did not. Dick, like himself, had rented his apartment by telephone, having been told by other actors that it was a convenient place to live. Like Fergus, Dick sent his rent cheques to a firm called Western Motor Homes, Inc.

'Exactly!' Fergus said, becoming excited. 'Our rental statements read, *Western Motor Homes, Inc., a division of Lompoc Industries, 1128 State Street, Lompoc, California.* The point I'm trying to make is that I've never met anyone from Lompoc Industries, or from Western Motor Homes, Inc. Mr Kane, who lives in Apartment Number One, is the janitor. At least, you apply to him when you first arrive, and you go to him if you lose your key. He arranges to have a new key made and delivered in a few hours by a company which makes keys. If there's any breakdown in my apartment, I phone Mr Kane, and he phones a service company. But – and this is the interesting part – Mr Kane is not, he tells me, an employee of Western Motor Homes. He has never met anyone from Western Motor Homes. He took over from the former janitor, who now lives in Pasadena and who was a friend of his. This job is just a part-time thing, he says. He gets an eighty per cent reduction in his rent by doing these chores. There is a paint and maintenance company which has the contract for maintenance and plumbing. There's a cleaning firm which sends these Mexican maids once a week to act as charwomen and change linen and bedding. It's all impersonal, don't you see? There's no busybody superintendent or concierge, as there is in New York or Paris. There are no neighbours who know who I am. I could be absent from this apartment for months, and as long as I sent the cheques to Western Motor Homes, Inc., in Lompoc, nobody would know that I was gone.'

'Wrong,' Dick Fowler said. 'There's me. I'd know.'

'Well, that's true,' Fergus admitted. 'But you don't really know my habits. You might think I'd gone East.'

'Man,' said Dick. 'You're getting all excited about this. But I still don't read you.'

'It's an interesting idea, though,' the girl said. 'I mean, the notion that places like this deny the existence of individuals.'

'But what's that got to do with him writing a book describing the furniture?' Dick asked.

'He's talking about the importance of the furniture's unimportance,' the girl said.

'I like that,' Dick Fowler said. 'It has an interesting sound. The importance of the furniture's unimportance. An interesting sound, goddammit!'

'Why do you find it interesting?' Fergus asked.

'It's the phrasing,' Dick said. 'It sounds like it has weight.'

Fergus and the girl burst out laughing, and it was in that minute, Fergus remembered, that he decided *he* was the one who should be dating her.

'What's so funny?' Dick asked.

'Fergus is talking about the meaning of things,' the girl said. 'You're talking about the sound of things. Now, that's another difference about California. People don't listen to what you're saying. It's how you *sound!*'

After that, Fergus remembered, Dick took us to a place called P.J.'s where he said the action was. But she and I were like children, giggling and making silly jokes. I suppose that's what's called love at first sight. Or pleasure. And a week later she was sitting in *my* efficiency apartment, drinking *my* margaritas, and to be fair to Dick, he held no grudge, he said I was in luck, and I was. Dani, unbelievably there, listening, as with the compulsive garrulity of the person who has been too much alone. I told and told, my past, my plans, and come to think of it, I knew nothing of her plans, nothing of her past except that she had studied sociology at UCLA and now worked for a computer firm, analysing materials. But what materials, and how did she analyse them? And that her mother was divorced and lived in Santa Monica. With her? Her father, she said, lived in San Francisco and was an exporter. But what did he export? She was so non-committal, so uncommitted, so different from any other girl I'd known, that when, suddenly, she went to bed with me, I was – what? Delighted, yes, but sure it couldn't last.

He looked at her now, across the room. He still could not be-lieve it. He remembered the day, four months ago, when the pair of them, searching for a lonely beach to picnic on, found this house in the dunes. Prowled around, saw the 'For Rent' sign, and when they got back to town, phoned the rental agent. He watched her now, stretching her body along the yellow sofa, her lion's mane of hair masking her face, the familiar, pleasant pain of his love mixed with a new fear, that these – what – apparitions? – would separate him from her. Not to worry, not to worry, he warned himself uselessly. It's just a temporary aberration – a day-mare! Not to worry, not to worry, they've gone.

But even as he told it to himself, sitting in this bright-lit room, the television set loud and reassuring, he sensed that they were back. They were in the house again. At once, he stood and stretched his arms, pretending to be tired.

'Yes,' Mrs Sinclair said, looking up from the television set. 'Beddy-byes. Me too.'

'You go ahead, Fergus,' Dani said. 'We'll be in in a minute.'

He nodded and smiled. Where were they? In which room?

'See you in the morning, Ferg,' Mrs Sinclair said. 'And thank you for a lovely evening.'

He went out into the brick-tiled corridor which led to the bed-rooms. Behind him, the television voices scrambled and faded, while, ahead of him, a new sound sent his head up, his step quickening as he went towards the back room, where Aunt Mary had been that morning. Over the voices, a sound of feet scraping, a sound of coughing. Was the kangaroo court in session? He hesitated.

The back-bedroom door was open. Moon lit the room. At first sight, despite the sounds, there was no one there. There was no one in sight because no one was standing, or even sitting: they were all kneeling – his father, his mother, Aunt Mary, his sisters Maeve and Kathleen, his young brother Jim. Kneeling, heads bowed, some at the bunk beds, some at the old chairs in this unused children's room. His father's voice sounding out: 'The third sorrowful Mystery, the Crowning with Thorns. Mary?'

Aunt Mary took an audible breath and began: 'Our Father, who art in heaven, hallowed be Thy name, Thy kingdom come, Thy will be done, on earth as it is in heaven.'

And the whole lot joining in: 'Give us this day our daily bread, and forgive us our trespasses, as we forgive those who trespass against us, and lead us not into temptation, but deliver us from evil. Amen.'

They were saying the family rosary.

Jim, his younger brother, was the only one who saw him. Jim, who seemed to be ten years old, was playing surreptitiously with a miniature car made out of a wooden matchbox, running the car along the counterpane of one of the bunk beds, at which he knelt.

'HAIL, Mary full of grace, the Lord is with thee. Blessed art thou amongst women, and blessed is the fruit of thy womb, Jesus,' Aunt Mary declaimed.

'HOLY Mary, mother of God,' the whole family joined in. 'Pray for us now and at the hour of our death, amen.'

'HAIL, Mary full of grace,' Aunt Mary began again, as Fergus, unnoticed by the others, knelt down beside Jim.

'Let's see your car?' Fergus whispered. He thought: Jim is thirty-six this year.

Jim, very pale, the skin on his childish face almost translucent, turned bright dark eyes on the man, and, tentative, offered the matchbox car. Fergus took it and looked at it. The matchbox advertised Swift's Blue Bird, a local match made long ago in Belfast. What should he say? Cool? Neat? Nice? He had forgotten the phrases of his boyhood. So nodded in silence, turning the car over, looking at the shirt-button wheels, axled to the box by women's hairpins. Jim looked on, uneasy, a child watching a strange man. 'I'm Fergus,' Fergus whispered. 'Don't you know me?'

'I have a brother called Fergus.'

'Holy Mary, mother of God, pray for us sinners, now and at the hour of our death, amen.'

'HAIL Mary, full of grace, the Lord is with thee –'

'That's me. I'm grown up,' Fergus whispered.

Jim stared at him, surprised, narrowing his eyes. Perhaps Jim was always shortsighted, Fergus decided, only we didn't notice it. 'You're joking me,' Jim whispered. 'You're not my brother.'

'I am. Don't you remember me grown up? The time we met in London? I was twenty-nine then.'

'In Chelsea,' Jim said. 'We got drunk.'

'Glory be to the Father and to the Son and to the Holy Ghost,' Aunt Mary declaimed. 'As it was in the beginning, is now and ever shall be, world without end. Amen.'

'If you're ten,' Fergus whispered, 'how do you remember what happened when you were twenty-nine?'

'The fourth sorrowful Mystery,' Dr Fadden announced. 'The Carrying of the Cross. Jim!'

'You never knew me after I was ten,' Jim whispered. 'We weren't friends from the time you went on to St Michan's.'

'Jim!' commanded Dr Fadden's voice, and Jim turned away from Fergus. 'Hail Mary full of grace,' Jim said, beginning to recite his decade of the rosary. Fergus, glancing back into the room, saw that the other members of the family still had their heads stuck into chairs and bunk beds and did not look in his direction. He waited until the family chorus took up the second part of the Hail Mary, then leaned towards Jim, whispering. 'Why weren't we friends?' But Jim shook his head at the impertinence of the question, as though Fergus should know full well, and Fergus did know: they had ceased to be friends because Fergus moved to a more grown-up school, and his new school friends did not want kids. Jim was always hanging around, wanting to play, wanting to go with them when they climbed Cave Hill. Fergus had to tell him to buzz off. From that time onward, Fergus thought our 'relationship', as they say out here, was over. He turned from Jim, who was racing through the Hail Marys as though he had a train to catch, and looked at the others. Kathleen, his second sister, who in reality was two years older than he, now knelt in prayer as a young woman, strangely garbed in what he first thought was an evening dress but realized was the

New Look of the early fifties. How dated she seemed, with her funny tight marcelled hair and very bright red lipstick and nail polish. Her clothes must be about nineteen-fifty-one, he decided, the year I finished university, the year she married Niall Nelligan, dour, righteous Niall, the archetypal brother-in-law, with his Brylcreem cowlick and Four-Square cut tobacco in the old Dunhill pipe, a porridge-faced Catholic Cotton Mather who was the end of her having anything more to do with me. It was over between us the day she married that praying mantis, down on their knees, the pair of them, saying the rosary at night before they got into bed to screw, oh, it would make you want to laugh if it didn't make you want to kick them. I haven't spoken to her or had a letter from her in – what? It must be fourteen years.

If Kathleen saw him, she paid no heed. As always, she was one of the few family members who didn't fidget at her prayers; she said them as though she meant them, head down, droning out the responses, a life of pious ejaculations, plenary indulgences, examinations of conscience, annual retreats, pilgrimages to the penitential station at Lough Derg with a holiday abroad, once every decade, to visit the shrine of Lourdes as a special treat. Yes, the generic Irish female of the sort who kept the priests in Powers' whiskey and Ireland the most distressful country, Europe's back of beyond. Old spleen curdled in him at thought of her and what she had become. He looked away.

But Maeve had seen him. She looked at him, a mischievous grin on her middle-aged face, recognizably kin to that sixteen-year-old Maeve with whom he had talked this morning. Well dressed, a confident Irish matron, she knelt uncomfortably on the hard floor, seemingly embarrassed by these devotions. Fergus winked at her, and she winked back. He must ask her where she had gone when she disappeared on the beach this morning. And *did* she speak to that fisherman?

'The fifth sorrowful Mystery, the Crucifixion,' Dr Fadden announced. 'Fergus!'

Were they asking him? Say your decade of the rosary, like a good fellow. By God, Fergus thought, and what if I do, just for fun, once again lead the prayers?

'Fergus?'

'That fellow.' It was Kathleen's voice. 'Oh, Daddy, sure isn't that fellow next door to a heathen? How would you expect prayers from the likes of him?'

'We'll see about that,' his father said. 'Fergus! I said the fifth sorrowful Mystery, the Crucifixion. Come along, now!'

'Our Father, who art in heaven,' Fergus began. 'Hallowed be Thy name –'

Kathleen rose to her feet. 'Daddy, I will not have a mockery made of the rosary!'

'What do you mean, miss?' Dr Fadden, in his serviceable striped, flannel pyjamas, woolly fleece-lined slippers, plaid, frogged Sherlock Holmes dressing gown, came up from the depths of his chair like an ostrich removing its head from sand.

'I mean – och, I'm ashamed to say it in front of the younger ones, but, Daddy, sure he's getting a *divorce*, it's a scandal, it doesn't bear repeating!'

'Divorce?' His father seemed puzzled. He looked at his wife. 'What *is* this, dear?'

Fergus's mother, who was kneeling next to Kathleen, reached up and tugged recalcitrant Kate back down on her knees. 'Are you not ashamed?' she whispered. 'Do you want your poor father to turn in his grave?'

'Oh!' Kathleen clapped her hand theatrically over her mouth as though to shut herself up. 'Oh, I forgot. Of course! Daddy never knew! God forgive me!'

'Fergus!' his mother hissed. 'Go on.'

'Give us this day our daily bread,' Fergus intoned. 'And forgive us our trespasses, as we forgive those who trespass against us.' (He looked at Kathleen as he said this.) 'And lead us not into temptation, but deliver us from evil, Amen.'

They all joined in as he finished the prayer, and now he went on easily to solo on the first half of the first Hail Mary. His father, satisfied, again went ostrich-head into his chair. And there in the moonlight, on the shores of the Pacific, kneeling in this unused back bedroom, Fergus led the dead and the absent living in his first prayers in twenty-five years: the Our Father, ten Hail Marys, and the Glory Be to the Father. It was as though he had never been away.

And when he had finished, his father, who had a lifetime devotion to Our Lady, wound up the rosary as always with the *Memorare*. It was a prayer which carried a plenary indulgence for the remission of sins. All, including Fergus, joined in, reciting it aloud.

'Remember, O most gracious Virgin Mary, that never was it known that anyone who fled to thy protection, implored thy help, or sought thy intercession, was left unaided. Inspired with this confidence, I fly unto thee, O virgin of virgins, my Mother: to thee I come, before thee I stand, sinful and sorrowful; O mother of the Word Incarnate, despise not my petitions; but in thy mercy hear and answer me. Amen.'

It really was wonderful, the most gorgeous piece of claptrap. The thought that it was still being solemnly intoned all over Ireland by bus drivers and bishops was enough to make Fergus burst out laughing. And now, as the members of his family finished the prayer in a mumbling dead heat, he thought of all the important things he had memorized and forgotten in his life. Yet he had remembered the *Memorare*.

All rose, as always after the family rosary, with alacrity and relief, all save Dr Fadden, who seemed to enjoy prayer, remaining on his knees for a last private afterword with God and an ostentatious Sign of the Cross, getting stiffly to his feet in the moonlight beside the bedraggled Mexican piñata paper donkey, which stood on the bound pile of ladies' magazines. Dr Fadden, puzzled, looked at the donkey, then said, 'Where's the wireless, dear? Did somebody move the wireless?'

'James, you're *not* in your own house,' Fergus's mother whispered.

'What?' His father looked around the room, confused, looking at Fergus but not seeming to see him, his face the face of a man on a dark road at night who discovers he has taken a wrong turning and is not sure anymore where he is. His father looked past Fergus, then saw something Fergus did not see, something which alarmed him, an alarm he tried to hide by reaching out his hand like a blind man, feeling for and finding the backrest of the rocking chair, steadying himself by touching it. His father's face, handsome in old age, with its heavy, curving moustache, a defiant lift to the jaw, and hurt, misunderstood eyes, was the face Fergus remembered. But what he did not remember was this look of uncertainty, an uncertainty which became something more sombre as his father, moving around the rocking chair, lowered himself carefully into it, and sat, slack, looking down at his slippered feet. His dead father, lost in some limbo of another world, sat in that very real rocking chair while his children, as they had in life, came up one by one to kiss their parent good night. Kathleen first, bending to peck her father's cheek, accepting his perfunctory hug and his 'Good night, dear,' then moving away to let Jim take her place, the same ritual, kiss, hug, and 'Good night, dear,' and then it was Maeve who said, 'Good night, Daddy,' and kissed her father with a touch of impatience, as though she were late for some appointment, and now it was Fergus's turn; he was the last – the others had already left the room; Aunt Mary and his mother must have hurried off to the kitchen to make the Ovaltine to carry upstairs in a thermos jug so that each of the children would be given a hot drink before being tucked in and the lights put out.

But there was no upstairs in this house. There was no wireless to comfort Dr Fadden with the nine-o'clock BBC news. His father sat in this anonymous house on the Pacific Ocean, six thousand miles from the Belfast that had been his home, staring past Fergus, seeing something Fergus did not see, his hands in the pockets of his frayed, frogged dressing gown, waiting for Fergus, an ageing son with thinning hair and drifting teeth, to bend and kiss his cheek and say good night as he had done every night until his father died. And there, in the moonlit children's room, with the night sea below on the beach, Fergus, nervous and trembling, bent to his filial duty, felt his lips touch the hard stubble on the old man's cheek, smelled the special smell which was his father, a smell of panatella cigars, Wills Gold Flake cigarettes, bay-rum hair tonic. Waiting for his father's 'Good night, son,' and the perfunctory hug before his father turned full attention to the perfidies of the world as reported by the British Broadcasting Corporation. But his father did not say good night, and his hug was not perfunctory. It was the hug of a person who does not want to let go.

'I'm cold,' his father said. 'Very cold. Do you think we could have the stove on?'

Fergus detached himself from his father's embrace. He went to the wall and turned on the central heating. 'Electric heat,' he said. 'It works very quickly.'

'Thank you,' his father said. He did not look at Fergus. He looked across the room at a back window which gave on the high bare mountains behind the house. 'Well,' said his father, 'are you happy?'

Fergus did not answer. He sat down opposite his father and tried to catch his eye. But his father looked through the window. His father looked at the mountains and sighed. 'I said, Are you happy?'

'Are you?' Fergus asked.

'Me?'

'Yes, you. Are you – in heaven?'

Dr Fadden did not answer for a while. Then said: 'Even the greatest saints of God are not without sin. Purgatory is a place or state in which souls suffer for a time after death, until they are purified from the effects of their sins. That is what the catechism says.'

'Then you are in purgatory, Daddy?'

Dr Fadden did not answer.

'If you are in purgatory, it means that, eventually, you will be admitted to heaven. So you must be happy about that?'

'Happy?' Dr Fadden said. 'Was I happy, did you say? In life? Was that what you asked?'

'Well,' said Fergus, 'I suppose we might begin with that.'

His father looked through the back window at the bare, high mountains behind the house. His father took his hands out of the pockets of his dressing gown and leaned forward in the rocking chair, knotting his fingers, concentrating as though he had been asked a question in an oral examination. 'Yes,' his father said. 'Happy? . . . I . . . I was fortunate to know some very fine men, men of sterling honesty and unfailing kindness, classmates of mine, many of them, yes, classmates at Michans in the old days . . . brilliant men; their scholastic records were, in many instances, outstanding. I was fortunate in my school friends, my friend John MacEoin, a man of European reputation in Celtic scholarship. But yes, yes, I have not yet answered the question. What was the question, it was, was it not, ah . . . was I happy . . . in life? Yes, that was it, that was the question. Well, in parentheses, may I be permitted a word of comment on my own academic career? My studies at Queen's College, Cork, and at the Royal Infirmary Medical School, Glasgow. Ahem! In 1910 I obtained a scholarship in anatomy, physiology, and surgery, an exhibition with first place and prize in midwifery, and first place and prize in medical jurisprudence. In 1915 I gained the Fellowship of the Royal College of Surgeons, Ireland. I . . . I mention this in passing, not out of any lack of modesty but merely to indicate that I derived some . . . some satisfaction . . . at the time. You asked the question was I happy in life, and to answer the first part of that question, in life there was some . . . some satisfaction from these and similar . . . but, yes, I realize I have not answered the question. *Happy*. Well, I remember one occasion in particular, a cycling holiday on the Continent, in France, as a matter of fact, we were four, my sister Kate, yes, before she entered the convent, and myself, and John MacEoin and Davy McAusley, he was a Bachelor of Laws – I remember we men had a rope-and-pulley attachment which we put on our bicycles and took turns pulling Kate uphill. At least, we were supposed to take turns, but we noticed, I mean, John and I noticed, that Davy was, well, ha, ha, that he had developed a great notion of Kate, and so we used to let him do all the work, pulling away like a carthorse, for she was a big girl, Kate, ha, ha, we shirked our turns, John and I, and let Davy . . . I don't know, for some reason it was very funny at the time. We laughed a great deal that summer. Beautiful weather it was, cycling all the way down to Provence. They say there is always good weather in the summer before a war. That was the summer of fourteen, remarkable weather, sunshine every day. I'll never forget it.'

'So, that summer you were happy,' Fergus said. 'Is that the only time you can think of?'

His father grew agitated, his fingers knotting and unknotting. He looked at Fergus, cleared his throat, and said deferentially, 'Yes, the . . . the question is a multi-part question, is it not, sir?'

He thinks I am an examiner, Fergus decided. He nodded to his father. 'That is correct.'

'Thank you, sir,' his father said. 'Now . . . happy . . . Ah, yes, now I have it! Yes . . . the answer. It was written of me, an encomium at the time, the time of my, hmm, demise, an encomium, one of several encomia – "encomia" is the plural, you see – one of many encomia written by friends and colleagues, the one I refer to in particular appeared in the *Irish News Letter* on the morning before the funeral, it said, and I quote: hmm: "As in all cases of true piety, Dr Fadden was not morose or sad. On the contrary, his acute observations of the humours of the persons he met in his large practice endowed him with a fund of good stories, which rendered him a most entertaining companion." Yes, that is what was written in the *Irish News Letter* by John MacEoin, one of my dearest friends, a man of European reputation in Celtic scholarship. And very well put, I think.'

His father paused, hopefully, smiling to himself, then looked at Fergus, waiting for Fergus's praise.

'Thank you,' Fergus said.

'Is that satisfactory, sir?'

'Well,' Fergus said, 'I suppose, as far as it goes. I mean, if that's as much as you can say?'

His father coughed, then rose, adjusting the skirts of his plaid dressing gown. 'No, no,' he said quietly. 'Not I. *You*. It is, perhaps, as much as *you* can say.'

'What do you mean?'

'It's not very difficult,' his father said. 'I'm sure that with reasonable application the meaning will become clear to you. Now, I'm going for a little turn outside. Good night, son.'

His father, brisk, walked across the room, opened the door, and stepped out. The door shut. It was an exit Fergus remembered. It mimed perfectly the startling change which used to come over his father each weekday afternoon when, putting aside his book in the upstairs sitting room, he went downstairs to his surgery to receive patients; the change which comes over an actor when he steps from the wings on stage, a new role in which Dr Fadden was no longer a paterfamilias, but, remote, forbidding, the senior surgeon in white coat, who, four days a week, walked the wards of the Mater Coeli Hospital, followed by his respectful outriders – residents, students, nurses, nuns. Of course, Fergus thought. That may be what he meant. After all, he was a surgeon; he saved lives. I never thought of that.

Fergus, hurrying, wanting to catch up with his father, went out of the unused back bedroom, hurrying down the corridor, going towards the outdoor terrace which overlooked the beach. Noticing, as he passed, that Mrs Sinclair was already in her bedroom; there was a light under her door. Meeting Dani, who came from the living room, tidying, plumping up cushions, switching off lamps.

'I thought you'd gone to bed already.'

'No,' he said.

Behind her, beyond the glass doors, out there on the terrace, a shadow moved past the chaise longue. His father taking a turn in the night air, as had been his custom in life.

'I want to shut the garage door,' Fergus lied.

'Okay. Then you put off the corridor light, right?'

'Fine.'

He went past her and opened the glass doors, looking back to make sure she went into their bedroom. He stepped out onto the terrace and saw his father, moving purposefully past the egg chairs, the chaise longue, and the group of deck chairs, going towards the bougainvillea bushes and the hidden playhouse. He pulled the glass doors shut so that Dani would not hear him.

'Daddy?' he called in a clear, carrying voice.

Dr Fadden whirled, the skirts of his dressing gown swirling. 'Shh!' he whispered, disapprovingly. 'Tch, tch, tch!'

'What's wrong?' Fergus asked.

'People are trying to sleep,' Dr Fadden said. 'What are you doing out here, anyway? You should have been in your bed long ago.'

So his father still saw him as a child, looked at him now in the moonlight and saw, not the grown-up man who had questioned him a few minutes ago, but a little boy who had been sent to bed with the other children after the family rosary; one spoke to children in a certain way, one must be firm. In his father's world there were rules: bed by ten, don't speak before you're spoken to, honour thy father and thy mother, remember thy last end. Children should be seen and not heard; certainly no latitude should be shown when a child who ought to be in bed is found to be out of doors late at night asking questions that are none of its business.

'Well, what *is* it?' his father said.

'Nothing.'

'Off you go, then! How can I be expected to get things arranged if you don't cooperate?'

'What things, Daddy?'

'You'll see,' Dr Fadden said crossly. 'A great deal of time and trouble has been taken on your behalf, a lot of people have had to put themselves out. It's been very difficult, it's not at all easy, let me tell you. Remember, the world isn't run just for your entertainment!'

'Daddy, what is all this, what are you talking about?'

'Tut, tut, tut, tut!' Dr Fadden said, finger upraised. 'That's enough. You'll find out when the time comes, don't you worry! Patience is a virtue that seems to be in short supply in your case, young man.' Peremptorily, Dr Fadden clapped his hands. 'B-E-D spells bed! Off you go! We'll call you.'

Then whirled away, going out of sight beyond the bougainvillea bushes. Behind Fergus a light went on at the side of the house. Dani, in their bathroom. He turned, went into the house, shut and locked the glass doors. What was being arranged, who were the people who 'had had to put themselves out' on his behalf? When would they call him, and for what? His heart started up again as he went into the bedroom, beating so quickly he was sure there must be something wrong organically, it couldn't just be nerves. He had read in *Newsweek* that more and more youngish men were having heart attacks nowadays, and that most first attacks were fatal.

'Are you all right?' Dani asked. She came to the bathroom door, toothbrush in hand.

'Fine,' said the man with the heart attack. His heart got the message and stopped beating so quickly. Dani turned away towards the bathroom mirror as Fergus began to undress. Undressing, he stared at her long, white, naked back, at the soft, fluctuant thighs, the red hair falling to her waist like a Victorian school-girl's mane. Vulnerable, unprotected. What help was he? Couldn't even protect himself. Let's face it, *amigo*, Boweri had said, you're in a very soft position. He had not phoned Boweri this evening, so his position was now very soft indeed. Tomorrow they would write him off. In the meantime, his dead father and these others were 'arranging' something for him. Was that something his death?

'Sure you're all right?' Dani asked, coming naked from the bathroom.

'Yes. Sure.'

'You look tired.'

'A good night's sleep,' he said. 'I mean, if I get a good night's sleep, then tomorrow I'll be okay, I'll put all this behind me. It will only be a memory.'

'What will?' she asked, confused.

'Hmm?' He looked at her. What had he said? 'Oh,' he lied. 'I meant Boweri and the film and all that. I'll be free of it by to-morrow.'

'Why? I don't understand.'

'I was supposed to call him tonight, remember? I mean if I agreed to make those changes.'

'Oh, yes,' Dani said. 'Well, you did the right thing. There are other jobs. Now, come on, let's get to bed.'

He went into the bathroom, washed his face, and brushed his teeth. He came back into the bedroom; she lay on her side of the bed, a sheet over her body, her eyes shut – vulnerable, unpro-tected. He got into bed and switched the light off, leaning over her. 'Good night, darling,' she murmured sleepily, as he kissed the nape of her neck, and moving close, spooned his body against her long back. Poor Dani, she'd be better off with anyone but him. What would she think if she knew how he had spent today? Apparitions, conversations with the absent and with the dead. Kneeling in the back room, reciting the rosary with ghosts. Per-haps this was how clinical madness began? Perhaps even Boweri was an apparition, perhaps Boweri never came here today, per-haps he had only imagined his talk with Boweri?

'Fergus?' Dani said sleepily. 'Your leg is twitching.'

'Sorry.' He turned away from her and lay, eyes open in the dark. Not twitching. Shivering. Why had these people appeared to him, what did they want. What did I do? he asked himself. What am I guilty of? What?

'Fergus, are you cold? You're shivering.'

He grunted negatively and moved to the other side of the bed. If Boweri was an apparition, if he never really came here today, then I'm done for. They will come for me. The men with the canvas waistcoats that tie in back. The men with the blue van.

He saw the van, the one that was pointed out to him as he came home from school down Elsworthy Avenue, long ago, the small blue van standing in the side street, unmarked, its attendants, men in grey uniforms from Purdysburn Mental Hospital, going in at the back door of a house to get Mr McGashan's old mother. People said she had a slate loose on top, she was round the bend, she had to be put away, the family couldn't cope anymore. An old woman Fergus had seen once in a park shelter during a shower of rain, led in there like an animal by her fat niece. He imagined the van, turning down off Pacific Coast Highway, coming down this driveway for him; watched it park in this moonlit driveway now as he floated on the edge of sleep; a blue van, small, unmarked, sinister. He slept.

Urinal etiquette forbade side-glancing the man standing next to you, although there were some, usually older men, who would do it. Shaking their members free of the last drops, they would glance over the porcelain barrier as though they had lost something, and in the process, sneak a quick look at your pecker. Very often this type of Nosy Parker was endowed in monstrous and disquieting fashion and would let you know it by withdrawing openly from the urinal at the end of the pee, unzipped, gripping some policeman's truncheon or genuine king-size Italian salami, a sight which made you wonder about all men being created equal.

As a rule, when he sensed that his neighbour was looking over the porcelain stall, Fergus moved directly to the attack, giving a sudden eyes-right, fixing the intruder in his stare, a move which usually returned the inquisitive one to a rigid atten-shun! eyes-front! This time, when his urinal neighbour (perceived subliminally as a stout, older person in a Navy pea jacket wearing some type of functionary's flat peaked cap), when this neighbour, shaking his member, sneaked a quick look over the wall, Fergus at once gave him the hard eye, what-are-you-a-fag-or-something routine, which did not faze this particular old part, who was Winston Spencer Churchill, dressed as an elder of Trinity Lighthouse, a Havana Monumental Perfecto Numero Uno in his jowl. Stepping back from the jakes, Churchill buttoned up his Navy pants, at the same time raising his left fist, fingers horned insultingly in the V for Victory sign, behaviour which Fergus accepted as normal, as he accepted Churchill, a familiar of his unconscious, whose appearance told him that this was no frightening daymare, but a normal night's dream.

He was not alarmed, therefore; but he was angry. Churchill headed Fergus's list of the Odious, Spurious Great.

'Fadden, isn't it?' queried the Former Naval Person. Fergus did not deign to answer. It was a favourite trick of old farts like Churchill to pretend they didn't remember you.

'Well?' said Churchill.

Fergus did not reply. Snubbed, Churchill plucked his cigar from his mouth and glowered in a passable imitation of the bulldog truculence shown in his famous portrait by Karsh of Ottawa.

'Oh, knock it off,' Fergus said, finishing up his own business and flushing his urinal.

'What? What?' Churchill seemed confused.

'That "they-shall-not-pass" look,' Fergus said. 'You weren't glaring at the enemy in that photograph, you were glaring because bloody little Karsh (you deserve him, by the way), because bloody little Karsh plucked the cigar out of your mouth so that he could snap your picture. Matter of fact, that story about Karsh and the cigar is a nice parable of your career, if you think about it.'

'What say?' Churchill seemed alarmed.

'The whole world saw you in that photo as the bulldog British leader, defending the free world against Hitler. When, in fact, all you were doing was pouting like a baby because somebody snatched your dummy tit.'

'Karsh of Ottawa,' Churchill said reminiscently. They were outside now, with no rhyme or reason to it, which was what was reassuring about dreams; they were walking down Park Lane on a foggy winter night, with some bloody great granite club façade in the background, and Churchill striding along beside Fergus, wearing his stovepipe topper and a heavy black Ulster cape. 'Have a brandy?' Churchill offered. 'Just a quick one,' Fergus said, and then they were in a pub, standing at the bar, the barman, a fellow with muttonchop whiskers, smiling and sucking up to Churchill, and the other people in the pub hanging back from the bar, nudging and staring, whispering and simpering, all of it surreptitious, all of them pretending not to notice Churchill (very English, that), and Churchill took his snout out of a great snifter of brandy and said, very seriously, tears glistening in his bulldog eyes, 'Let us therefore brace ourselves to our duty, so bear ourselves, that if the British Empire and its Commonwealth last for a thousand years, men will still say – *this* – was their finest hour!'

'Ballocks,' Fergus told him. 'A thousand years from now, with experimental cities on the moon and maybe two thermonuclear wars behind us, I doubt very much if they'll remember you any more than they'll remember Bismarck. Hyperbole, that was always your trouble. In your writing, too. Of course, your style of sermonizing suits that ham-actor pulpit voice you cultivated. As for your writing, you wrote like a Presbyterian minister.'

'I won the Nobel Prize,' Churchill said.

'Not for literature,' Fergus said. 'That's typical of you. Half-truths and half-lies.'

'Arrest him,' Churchill said, turning to the barman. The barman blew a police whistle. London bobbies in old-fashioned helmets rushed into the pub in a flying wedge, took hold of Fergus's hands, and handcuffed him. 'Get the darbies on,' cried one. 'Fookin' Irish get,' said another in a Yorkshire accent. A third policeman, a sergeant, winked at the pub crowd. 'You go in the cell with them, see,' said he. 'Reach over like this, see. Pull down 'ard on Paddy's balls. Leaves no marks, see.'

Smiling, the sergeant jerked on Fergus's testicles. Fergus moaned. The people in the pub crowded around laughing.

'Home rule,' Churchill said. 'I supported Home Rule.'

'Because it suited you,' Fergus said. 'But you were a wog-hater at heart.'

Churchill twirled his Ulster cape. 'Battle of Sydney Street,' he rumbled. 'I put those strikers in their place. Hit him!'

One of the bobbies smashed Fergus across the nose. The pub crowd applauded. 'Well played, sir. Good shot. Hit him for six!'

'Look at this man's record,' Churchill told the crowd. 'Chronically late for school, failed his examinations. Not qualified to be anything other than a pen-pushing clerk. Writer, pah! Drifter! Give 'em a chance to make something of themselves, and they can't even be trusted to turn out a simple film script. Unfit as a parent. Wife put detectives on him. Sordid! Desertion is desertion, no two ways about it. Bad blood. Now he's seeing things. Fact. Talks to himself out loud. Need I go on?'

'Bonkers!' someone shouted.

'Exactly,' Churchill said. 'Lock him up!'

The bobbies, shoving and pushing, began to drag Fergus towards the pub door. Outside, he could see the blue van, in a side street. Small, unmarked. 'No, please!' Fergus screamed. 'Please, I'm sorry, please listen to me, I didn't mean any harm, I won't be late anymore, I'll be in before nine every morning, I'll study, I'll pass every test, every subject in my exams –'

'Stow it, Paddy,' said a bobby. 'You're wasting breath. "Life imprisonment," the judge said.'

'No sentence,' Churchill called from the bar of the pub. 'Incompetent to stand trial. Institution, I recommend. Hah? Throw away the key.'

'Very good, sir,' the sergeant said, saluting. 'Come along, you. Best go quietly.'

The van, he saw the van, he tried to dig his heels into the stoop at the threshold of the pub, but Churchill, coming up behind the police, kicked him in the ankles, making him stumble and fall forward. The police rushed him out into the street. The men in grey uniforms were waiting, holding the straitjacket, stiff canvas, its long laces dangling. 'I'll sign the papers,' Churchill told them.

'You're not a doctor!' Fergus twisted around, screaming, trying to appeal to the pub crowd.

'Order of her Majesty's government,' Churchill said. He was

dressed as a Knight of the Garter and looked like an old lady got up for a garden party. He read from a parchment scroll. 'Taken from here to a place of confinement, there to remain for the remainder of his natural days . . . Hmm. Seems in order.' He signed with a flourish of a quill pen.

'Thank you, sir,' said one of the asylum attendants, taking the paper, saluting Churchill.

The policemen lifted Fergus into the dark van. He screamed, screamed. They were pulling him about. It was dark, and someone was pulling on his shoulder, and he was in bed, awake. The light went on. Dani, pulling at him, staring. 'Wow!' she said. 'You scared hell out of me.'

Stupid, Fergus looked at her; there was no blue van, no police, dream; he –

'Are you all right?' A woman's voice from the other room.

'Yes, Ma, go back to sleep,' Dani called. She smiled at Fergus. 'She'll think I'm choking you. You yelling like that.'

'Sorry,' Fergus said. 'I had a bad dream.'

Dani lay down, drawing the covers up to her chin. 'That's all right, baby. Go to sleep.' She reached for the light pull by her bed. The room went black.

Fergus lay on his side and took a deep breath, which became a yawn. Almost immediately, he was startled by a loud noise outside in the corridor.

'Christ!' said Mrs Sinclair's voice.

'Ma? Are you all right?' Dani called.

'I'm fine, hon. I'm looking for a glass of water.'

'Wait a minute,' Dani said, beginning to rise in the bed.

'I'll go,' Fergus said.

'No, I will.'

'No,' Fergus said. 'You go back to sleep.'

He sat up, slid his feet into his slippers, and went out into the moonlit corridor, where Mrs Sinclair, moving uncertainly along the wall, groping for a light switch, revealed herself as Fergus switched on the light, tall, spectral in a white batiste nightgown with lace ruffles at wrist and neck, and a white cotton peignoir, the whole topped by a strange pink-petalled mobcap which sat like an inverted artichoke on her head. 'Oh, there you are,' Mrs Sinclair said, blinking. 'I didn't mean to, I didn't want to bother you. But I have this terrible thirsty feeling.'

'I woke you,' Fergus said. 'Yelling in my sleep.'

'No, no, I'm a very light sleeper, always was. Now, please don't disturb yourself, go back to bed. I can manage, now I have the light, it was looking for the light I knocked over that goddam pot there.' Smiling apologetically, still seeming half-asleep, her face partially erased, eyebrows blurred, lips bare and bloodless.

'No,' Fergus said. 'Now that I'm up, let me get you something. What would you like?'

'Oh, I guess a Coke would be nice.'

'A Coke,' Fergus said. He moved past her, going towards the kitchen.

'Well, ah, wait a minute, no, I think, I tell you what, maybe I'll have a nightcap, a good stiff Scotch on the rocks, that might knock me out, put me right back to sleep, is that okay?'

'Of course. Scotch on the rocks.' Fergus made a right turn in the direction of the living room. He switched on the lamp by the table where the drinks were kept, and as he did, looked in turn at each corner of the room to be sure they were alone. He listened for voices. Below, on the beach, waves broke on the sands, loud, continuous, for ever and ever, amen. Mrs Sinclair was offering him a cigarette. He smiled and shook his head.

With an uncertain aim, long-sightedly, she put her lighter flame up, searching for the tip of her cigarette. As the lighter clicked shut, Fergus poured a large measure of Scotch, then poured a second for himself. He no longer enjoyed getting drunk, but remembering his drinking days, knew that his joining her would please his guest. 'Cheers,' he said, handing her a glass, raising his own glass. Mrs Sinclair smiled vaguely, tasted her drink, then, cradling it with both hands, moved across the living room to settle on a small footstool with something of the awkward gathering and squatting movements of a swan settling on dry land. Swan in white lace ruffles, petalled pink mobcap, white batiste falling back to show the tanned dark skin of her long, thin forearms and the dark tendons in her long throat, she peered up blindly into the lamplight, looking past its brightness at where she imagined Fergus stood, saying conversationally, 'Isn't Dani a great kid?'

'She is.'

'I have a son, did you know?'

'No, I didn't.'

'He's retarded. He's in an institution. I worried so much when Dani was born, but, well, she's just fine, isn't she?'

'She certainly is,' Fergus said. His Scotch tasted oily. He put some water in it.

'I mean, she's so creative. I don't know, she's really so – so sensitive and talented, and yet all the time such a wonderful, well, just a great human being.'

'A person is what they do. A man is what he does, not what he says he does. Right, lads?'

Paddy Donlon's voice, that knowing voice from the back room of a pub, that voice which had accused him this afternoon in the kangaroo-court session. The burn of the whiskey caught at Fergus's throat, making him cough. Under pretence of diverting his cough from Mrs Sinclair's direction, he turned his head away, looking down at the far end of the room, where, in the dining alcove, sitting at the round, mahogany dining table, as easy as if he were in the back room of Gallagher's Lounge, Patrick Sarsfield Donlon looked over at Fergus; tall, boyish, with a brilliantined curl falling over his forehead, a full, sensual lower lip twisting in a mocker's grin. Jokey, serious Paddy, who once sat in judgement on himself and all his friends over pints of Guinness's porter in the back room of Gallagher's Lounge. *A man is what he does.* The wisdom of the pub.

'Of course, I guess that's one of the reasons she respects *you*,' Mrs Sinclair said. 'She always had great respect for creative people. You should hear her about Frank Sinatra.'

'Ah, Sinathra,' said Paddy, nodding his head. 'Now, *there* is a creative member. Very, very creative, right enough.'

Mrs Sinclair rose from her footstool, swayed, steadied herself by leaning against the back of the orange armchair, then went purposefully towards the drinks table. Ice clinked in her glass.

'Of course, she's not, you know, she's not smart about men, that little girl.' Mrs Sinclair held her glass against the light, measuring its contents. 'Well, maybe just a touch of Scotch in this to freshen it up, okay?'

'Carry on.'

'What about you? Need a refill?'

'Thanks,' Fergus said. He rose and offered his glass. Mrs Sinclair, shifting her grip to hold the bottle by its base, inexpertly slopped a large measure of Scotch into his drink. 'When I was her age, I wanted to get married. But kids nowadays, they don't care . . . Dani says you can't get a divorce. Is that right?'

'No, no, my lawyer's working on it. Something's going to give. Soon, I hope. You know what these things are like.'

'I certainly do,' Mrs Sinclair said. She sat on the yellow sofa and stirred her drink with her finger. Fergus looked at the dining alcove. Paddy had turned his back to them and was facing the dark wall.

Mrs Sinclair looked into her drink, then sipped it. 'Women fight dirty in a divorce,' she said. 'Some women. I never did. Not with either of my husbands. But some women. I have stories would take your hair off. Yes.'

In the shadows at the far end of the room Paddy Donlon sat, staring at the wall. He cradled his pint of porter, but the porter was barely sipped. 'I had a friend once,' Fergus said, speaking loudly so that his voice would carry through the room. 'A friend back in Ireland when I was going to the university. A medical student. He used to say that a man is what he does, not what he says he does. I was thinking of that just now, when you asked me if I want a divorce.'

'I didn't ask you that,' Mrs Sinclair said. 'I didn't say "want."'

'But that's what you meant?'

'Yes, I guess it is.'

'Well, I do want a divorce. But I have to prove it, don't I? I mean, to Dani.'

'To Dani? Oh, I don't know.' Mrs Sinclair looked again at her drink. 'I don't know what Dani wants. Do you?'

'No, I suppose I don't.'

'I mean, I know she likes you. Likes you a lot, as a guy, you know? But, she's, ah, she's different from the rest of us. What was it your friend said – the student?'

'A man is what he does. Not what he says he does.'

'Yes, that could be. It could be,' Mrs Sinclair said slowly. She raised her head and looked at Fergus across the pool of yellow light cast by the table lamp. Her eyes were moist. 'But then, some people can't do what they wish to do. You know?' She blinked, and tears formed on her lower eyelashes. 'I mean, I can't always do what I wish to do.' She held up the drink, putting her glass against the light as though it were a laboratory sample. 'I mean, I'd like to give this up.' She lowered the glass and stared at Fergus. 'Your friend would say that doesn't count. But I figure a person, well, a person deserves some credit for trying. Don't you think?'

Fergus looked at the dining alcove. Paddy sat with his back to them. 'My friend would have understood that,' Fergus said. 'He was a drinking man himself.'

'Your friend,' Mrs Sinclair said. 'Did he, I mean, did he pass on?'

'Yes,' said Fergus.

He had received the clipping in New York, inserted illegally (as was her habit) into a blue airmail-letter form sent by his mother. When she put something in an air-letter form (which was forbidden by Post Office regulations), she would never mention the enclosure in the accompanying letter, because she believed that to do so would render her liable to prosecution. Thus the small obituary notice in the paid 'Births and Deaths' column of the *Irish News Letter* was not supplemented by any further details. *DEATH: 27 January: Patrick Sarsfield Donlon, M.B., only son of Terence and Delia (Gilrooney). In Cawnpore, India, in his twenty-fifth year. May He Rest in Peace.* Typhus was the story his parents put about, and drink was what some people might say, but Rory Pakenham, who was in India with the World Health Service, told Fergus's sister Maeve that there was an inquest and a verdict of suicide. Paddy put a revolver in his mouth and pulled the trigger, Rory said. *A man is what he does.* And so, years ago, Paddy, drinking porter in the back room of Gallagher's Lounge, all unknowing, pronounced his epitaph. Revolver, trigger, bullet, blood. When he first qualified as a doctor, Paddy went to do a *locum tenens* for a doctor in Cork. There, drunk, some said, he drove away one night from a friend's house and ran over and killed a girl. The courts were kind; the manslaughter charge was dismissed. Acquitted, Paddy did the decent thing. He left Ireland. And, a year later, sentenced himself in Cawnpore, India. Patrick Sarsfield Donlon. Fergus looked at Paddy's unmoving back, there in the alcove, then looked again at Mrs Sinclair, who raised the Scotch to her lips, hesitated before drinking, and said, 'I'm sorry.'

'Sorry?'

'About your friend, passing on.'

'Aye. Sorry for my trouble, missis,' said Paddy's drunk voice from the other end of the room. Fergus, glancing surreptitiously over his shoulder, saw that Paddy had turned away from the wall and now sat facing them, raising his pint of porter in mock salutation. 'Fergus,' said Paddy, 'do you remember the night we burned the Holy Ghost?'

Uneasy, Fergus turned from Paddy's grinning face. I am not going to answer direct questions from these apparitions in the presence of real people. That's what mad people do: talk to persons who aren't there.

'Fergus, did you hear me?' Paddy insisted.

'What?' Fergus said, confused, trapped into speech, but pretending he did not understand.

'Your friend,' Mrs Sinclair said. 'The one who died.'

'The Holy Ghost,' Paddy said. 'D'you remember, it was a New Year's Eve, and the pair of us had been at that party in the nurses' quarters at the old Mater Coeli Hospital, and we were coming home, all boozed up, alone in the street in the middle of the night, and didn't there come a piece of newspaper blowing along the street, and you trapped it with your foot and picked it up and started tearing circles of newspaper out and holding them up like communion hosts and praying over them, saying the responses to the Mass and then burning the bits of paper with your cigarette lighter, watching them go up in flames and ashes, the pair of us drunk as lords there in the Cliftonville Road, and you on your knees making mock of God. Oh, you were the wild bloody man, in those days.'

'You always said that about me,' Fergus told Paddy. 'But it's not true.'

'You mean he didn't die?' Mrs Sinclair asked.

'No, you were wild, all right,' Paddy told Fergus. 'Always up to lunatic tricks. God, you scared me that night. There you were, kneeling, blaspheming in the street, when this bloody great policeman comes around the corner, and says he, "What the hell do you think you're doing?" and says you, "I'm elevating the *Irish News Letter* to the status of the Godhead." Jaysus, I thought he was going to put you in a straitjacket.'

'But I don't remember it,' Fergus said. 'When a thing is told to you and you can't remember it happening, it doesn't count, somehow. It's as though it had nothing to do with you. Remembering, that's what counts.'

'I know,' Mrs Sinclair said. 'Sometimes it's hard to believe that people you knew are dead. When you remember them, so alive.'

'I'm sorry,' Fergus said to Mrs Sinclair. 'I'm afraid I was rambling on, there. Talking to myself.' He laughed uneasily.

'That's okay, Fergie. I just misunderstood you, that's all.'

In the alcove, Paddy shook his head. 'Funny, you don't remember that night,' he said. 'If ever I thought of you, Fergus Fadden, that was the night I remembered you by.'

'I know,' Fergus said, trapped once again in the cross-talk of conversation. 'Funny, isn't it, the times a person *does* remember. Do you remember the night we met Gildea?'

'Gildea?' Mrs Sinclair asked. 'Who's he? Oh, Fergie, I think you've got a little bun on.'

'Gildea. The so-called bard,' Paddy said. 'Your man with the beard.'

'That's right,' Fergus said.

'Well, good for you,' Mrs Sinclair said, smiling, holding up her glass in toast to Fergus. 'Let me tell you something,' she said. 'I'm a little smashed myself.'

'He's dead now, you know,' Paddy said. 'He emigrated to

America and got hooked in by the American Air Force. He went to Korea.'

'You're kidding?' Fergus said.

'No, he was a pilot,' Paddy said. 'His plane went down in the China Sea.'

'No, no kidding,' Mrs Sinclair said. 'I've got a bun on.'

'But, it's funny,' Fergus said, looking first at Mrs Sinclair, then at Paddy. 'I mean, it's funny the things you *do* remember. There was an evening long ago . . . it seemed to me terribly significant at the time. When I think of Hugh Gildea, I always think of that night.'

'You mean your friend who died?' Mrs Sinclair asked.

'Yes,' Fergus said. He looked over at Paddy. He would tell Paddy the story while pretending to tell it to Mrs Sinclair. 'This night I remember,' he said. 'It was years ago. I was with my best friend, a fellow by the name of Paddy Donlon.' In the dining alcove, Paddy shook his head. 'Get away with you!' Paddy said. 'You had all classifications of friends. Stop trying to butter me up.'

'Anyway,' Fergus said, looking back at Mrs Sinclair, 'my friend and I had taken two girls to the pictures –'

'Do you mean the movies?'

'Yes. And after we saw the girls home we went for a few drinks to a pub called The Hole in the Wall.'

'The Hole in the Wall,' Mrs Sinclair said. 'You British certainly have some cute names for your "pubs". Do you know a place in Santa Monica called Ye Mucky Duck?' She laughed.

'Anyway,' Fergus said, 'when we came out of this place, there were four or five of us, it must have been after midnight. We started off up Dunsmere Avenue, and there was your man, Gildea. He was walking a sentry-go up and down outside a house on the opposite side of the avenue. I could see him under the streetlamp, and although I didn't know him, I knew who he was. I'd been told he was a poet. He had a black beard; he looked a bit like D. H. Lawrence. But anyway, there he was walking up and down on sentry duty, and when one of our fellows asked him what he was doing, he said he'd been thrown out of this house a few minutes ago. Seems he was in bed with this girl when her parents came home, and the girl's father was a Presbyterian minister, no less –'

'Oh, my!' interjected Mrs Sinclair.

'Anyway, the father had just thrown Gildea out of the house and warned him that if ever he spoke to his daughter again, he, the father, would put the police on Gildea, and there was your man Gildea, not taking that lying down, but wanting revenge, and suddenly he starts shouting up at the house: "Come on out, come on out, the pair of you. Old Mortality and Sergeant Death!" Old Mortality was his name for the father, and Sergeant Death was what he called the mother. Do you not remember, now?'

'No,' said Paddy. 'Not that night. I remember he was a wild man, though. But no butty of mine. A stuck-up Protestant get, he was. A Catholic, to him, was dirt.'

'Old Mortality,' Mrs Sinclair said, and giggled. 'It *is* kind of a good name for a minister.'

'Anyway,' said Fergus, 'there was Gildea standing under the streetlamp in a quiet avenue at midnight, shouting up at this house, and when we went over, he asked us to shout too, and we did, and I remember yelling, "Come out of there, Old Mortality!" and then, I remember I nearly stiffened with fright when Old Mortality himself opened the front door in his minister's collar and black suit, and points the finger right at us. "I just want to inform you hooligans that I have telephoned the police. They'll be here shortly." Then, as the old minister made to shut the front door, Gildea rushed up the path, shouting, "Just a minute, just a minute, Reverend!" And stopped there on the path, pulling a tin toy out of his pocket. Now, do you not remember?'

Paddy Donlon shook his head. No.

Mrs Sinclair, smiling vaguely, said, 'It was somebody else you told it to. But go on, it's very interesting.'

'Anyway, with everybody, including the old minister, watching, Gildea squatted on the path, put the tin toy on the flagstones, and wound up the key in its back. It was one of those little tin men that street hawkers used to sell off a tray. And Gildea looked up at the minister standing there in the front doorway of that house in Dunsmere Avenue in Belfast, and said Gildea to the minister,

"Watch this." And let go of the toy, and the toy started to go tick-tick-tick, going around in a circle on the flagstones of the minister's front path. And Gildea stood up, looked down at the toy and recited:

'The tin toys of the hawker move on the pavement, inch by inch
Not knowing they are wound up: it is better to be so.
Than to be like us, wound up and while running down to know –'

'And, with that, the old minister slammed his front door shut, and the rest of us, afraid that the police were on the way, dodged off and left Gildea there on the path. I remember looking back, and he was standing, watching the toy going around and around. And when it stopped, he picked it up and put it in his pocket and just stood there as though he were waiting for the police. He wouldn't run away, you see. And it started to rain, and we left him there. It seemed meaningful to me. At the time, I thought it was his own poem.'

'It was Louis MacNeice who wrote it,' Paddy said.

'I know. You were the one who told me that.'

'Told you what?' Mrs Sinclair asked.

'Gildea was a posturing bloody twit of a man,' Paddy said. 'Poet, my arse.'

'But to me he seemed a poet,' Fergus said. 'I was nineteen. I'd never known any poets, and he seemed different, he had a different way of behaving from the rest of us. That's the important thing. It doesn't matter what he wrote or what he did. It's what *I* thought he wrote and did, that's what counted for me. It's what still counts. For me. When I think back and remember people who had an influence on me, he – Gildea – is one of those people. Not because of what he wrote or did, but because of what he seemed to have done. Yes, that's it. Because of what he *seemed* to have done.'

'A man is what he *does*,' Paddy said.

Mrs Sinclair nodded. 'Yes, I think I know what you mean, Fergie. Some people, well, they're just fantastic human beings, they, well, they give off something like sound waves, you can't help coming under their influence. You know who was like that? Aimee Semple McPherson. I knew her, did I tell you? I was just a kid, I used to sing in the choir at her temple. She was *something!*'

But Fergus did not want to hear about Aimee Semple McPherson. 'Anyway,' he said, looking past Mrs Sinclair, looking at Paddy, who had finished his pint and was lighting a Woodbine cigarette, 'the thing is,' Fergus told Paddy, 'you remember me on a particular night, I remember Hugh Gildea because of another particular night. Both of us – Gildea and I – acting like lunatics. Is it only when people are a bit mad that they seem memorable? We remember so damned little, don't we?'

Paddy cocked a forefinger and thumb, shaping his hand like a pistol. He opened his mouth and pointed his forefinger at it. 'Bang!' he said. 'Memory close the door.' He laughed.

'Yes, I know,' Mrs Sinclair said. 'It's awful, isn't it, how you forget things? You know this stuff, the Scotches and the martinis, that's what does it to you, brother, does it ever! You know, Fergie, I'm going to do something about it, I'm really going to try this time. I'll go to UCLA this year and study Spanish, or painting, or art appreciation, or something. I've got to get myself involved in a mind project. You know?'

Paddy stood up, moving out from the darkened dining alcove, his cigarette cheap as a wilted toothpick in his mouth. He winked, his brilliantined curls falling childlike over his right eye. 'Why don't we dodge outside?' he said. 'And give old Aimee Semple the slip?'

Fergus, nodding to show Paddy he understood, rose and smiled at Mrs Sinclair. He put his empty glass down on the drinks table, saying, 'I must get back to bed.'

'Yes,' Mrs Sinclair said. 'It's late. I think, though, that I'll just finish this up. You go ahead, hon. And thank you for your company.'

Fergus, moving to the glass doors, opened them, allowing Paddy to go past him onto the moonlit terrace.

'You going outside?' Mrs Sinclair asked, trying to shade her eyes, peering blindly through the pool of light from the table lamp.

'Just want to check on the garage door. Good night, Mrs Sinclair. Sleep well.'

'Dusty!'

'Sorry. Dusty.'

'Good night, Fergie. Take care.'

'Good night.' Fergus stepped outside, shutting the glass doors. Paddy waited in the moonlight, lighting a new cigarette from the butt of his old one. 'Not so Dusty,' Paddy said, and laughed. 'Are there any more at home like her?'

'She's my girl friend's mother.'

'Aren't you the terrible, bloody man! Girl friend! And what age is the girl friend?'

'You know. So why ask?'

'I do not. I never met her.'

'She's twenty-two.'

'Is she, now? And yourself?'

'Thirty-nine.'

'The real Sugar Daddy.'

'Sugar Daddy!' Fergus said. 'Even the phrase is archaic. Shows how out-of-date you are.'

'I am that,' Paddy said. 'I died in fifty-one.'

'Yes, I forgot.'

'No, you didn't, Fergus,' Paddy said. 'It's the one thing you remember about me.'

A suicide, Rory Pakenham had said. Fergus looked at Paddy, who made a catapulting motion with his finger and thumb, projecting the butt of his used Woodbine cigarette in a fiery parabola up in the air, to fall beyond the terrace into the bank of rubbery ice plant. Below the bank, moonlight whitened the strand, and the breakers, beginning their curl, rounded into long bar rails of glinting silver before crashing on the beach, their great strength smashed into smithereens. Paddy Donlon stood, staring at the sea, wearing the clothes of twenty years ago, an ill-fitting jacket of Irish tweed, the side pockets lumpy with concealed objects, a blue-and-white-striped shirt, its long collar points curling like wilted leaves, a striped Irish poplin tie, unpressed flannel trousers, battered brown brogues. Paddy, stage-lit by that brilliant moonlight, young, grubby, seeming to smell of hops from the porter he had drunk and the urinal stink of the cheap cigarettes he smoked. Paddy, dead of his own hand.

Paddy turned from his contemplation of the seascape. 'Well, young fellow-me-lad,' he said, mimicking the slight stammer of Tiny Kelly, their geography master at St Michans. 'Well, now, and so you became a – a scrivener, after all. On my soul, you did! A– a – scrivener!'

'Tiny!' Fergus began to laugh. 'I haven't thought of him for years!'

'What a bunch of comedians they were!'

'Tiny Kelly, Stinks Garvey in science, Froggy Pusey for French–'

'And old Billie Burke!'

'Father Daniel Aloysius Burke. I am the Dean of Discipline, sonny boy. Do you know what that means?'

Laughing, Fergus faced Paddy, who, laughing, was falling about on the terrace, blundering into the chaise longue. 'Sonny boy!' Paddy cried.

'It's a wonder we learned anything at all!'

'Aye, but what did we learn? What did they know? Do you remember Froggy Pusey's French accent?'

'Didn't I have cause to, the first time I was in France?' Fergus cried. 'I swear there's no Frenchman, now or ever, who could understand him.'

'Froggy,' Paddy said. 'Even their nicknames were unoriginal.'

'School nicknames are,' Fergus said. 'They have to be, to last, year after year, class after class.'

'God,' Paddy said. 'How I remember my first week in that school. All I knew was, I was away from my Mammy and put in a madhouse.'

'But nicknames helped. They made the monsters comic.'

'Comic, sir? Did you say comic? What do you mean, sir? Explain yourself, sir!' Paddy cried, in the tones of Father Billie Burke.

'I shall try, sir,' Fergus answered. 'My first proposition is that schoolboys are children. Children see adults as caricatures. Schoolmasters soon learn that boys remember them for eccentricities of dress, behaviour, speech. Schoolmasters exaggerate these eccentricities in order to create a classroom persona. And, for most schoolmasters, their eccentricities become a large part of their teaching performance. We remember schoolmasters as we remember actors. And certain pieces of learning stay in our minds as the tag lines of academic comedians.'

'Well put, sir, well put,' Paddy said, laughing. 'You're a – a – scrivener to your fingertips.'

'And yourself, your honour, sure, didn't you become a doctor?' Fergus said. 'Ah, yes, as Tiny would say, you became – a – a sawbones!'

'A sawbones. Right! Right indeed, sir!'

'So even *we* have become caricatures,' Fergus said. 'The scrivener and the sawbones.'

'Are you surprised?' Paddy asked. 'Isn't that all any of us are, when other people bring us to mind? Caricatures!'

'I know,' Fergus said. 'There's got to be more to my father, for instance, than that joke figure who popped up in the armchair this morning.'

Paddy stared at the sea. 'Funny,' he said. 'If the parents we remember aren't our real parents at all. Just our childish misconceptions about them.'

'Jesus!' Excited, Fergus began to pace up and down on the terrace. 'Maybe you've got something. Maybe that's why my parents have come back: maybe after what happened today, those masks I put on them for so many years will fall away and I'll see my parents as they really were! I'll stop blaming and misjudging them as I did when I was a kid? By God, Paddy, maybe that's it! They're trying to reveal themselves to me!'

Paddy lit the last Woodbine cigarette from his package, and crumpling the package, threw it into the ice plant. 'Could be. But there's the converse possibility, as Stinks Garvey would say.'

'What converse?'

'The converse is, because children feel weak and need reassurance, they tend to project onto their parents their own hopes and fantasies of being powerful, wise, and good. If your parents come back now, freed by time, they risk that you see them, not as an adoring child, but as a dispassionate adult. Do you see? Your real parents may have been smaller, duller, and less intelligent than those "parents" who live on in your memory?'

'Yes, that could be,' Fergus said. 'You're right, it's not in human nature to prune the family tree.'

'Legends,' Paddy said. He stood, dragging on his cigarette until it burned coal bright in the moonlight. Then faced Fergus, his eyes grave, his boyish curls blowing about his brow. 'A man is what he does, not what he says he does, eh, Fergus? That's still true, isn't it?'

'I don't know. Legends can become facts.'

'Aye, especially if they make a better story than the facts do,' Paddy said. 'You know what I'm talking about, don't you?'

Fergus was silent.

'Tell me,' said Paddy. 'Do *you* think I put a gun in my mouth and blew my brains out?'

'I suppose I do.'

'Well, that's the answer. You think it, therefore I did it. And you *want* to think it, because it's dramatic. It makes a good story, doesn't it?'

'I suppose so.'

'The lousy truth,' Paddy said, 'is that it's the one thing you'll always remember when you remember me. Paddy Donlon blew his brains out in Cawnpore. Guilty Paddy Donlon.'

'That's not all I remember,' Fergus said. 'I remember us together at Queens, I remember us in pubs, I remember our jokes. I remember walking along the Lagan River talking to you.'

'You remember me as saying that a man is what he does, not what he says he does. And that I blew my head off. I can't blame you,' Paddy said. 'I *am* a bloody caricature after all.'

'Paddy,' Fergus said, 'I miss you.'

'Shut up,' Paddy said. He turned from Fergus and ran, across the terrace and down the dirt steps leading to the beach, the run of a boy of twenty, reckless, jumping three steps at a time, as Fergus, following him, began to run too, running after Paddy, who, his tweed jacket open, his long necktie fluttering behind him, gathered himself and leaped from the dune to the beach, crouching as he landed, then ran across the sands towards the breakers which rolled in, strong, slow, smashing in silver shards on the shore. Fergus, running, winded, feeling his years, came to the edge of the dune, jumped, although he knew he shouldn't, and fell heavily on his hands and knees in the sand. On all fours, panting, too old for these boyish antics, missing a sandal. Scrabbling in the sand, he located the sandal, then sat, putting it on. Someone stood over him.

It was not Paddy. A slight young man in check tweeds, silly polka-dot tie, straight-stemmed pipe held in his hand like a stage prop.

'Where's Paddy?' Fergus asked his younger self, who puffed on the pipe with a nonchalance which Fergus, more than any other person in the world, could at once detect as false. Fergus looked at this apparition; it occurred to him that some of these ghosts might fear him.

'I asked you a question.'

His young self removed the pipe, gesticulating with it, dismissing the question. 'He's not here. Sure, the man's dead and buried.'

'I know he's dead,' Fergus shouted. 'For God's sake! Always the bloody obvious! I know Paddy's dead. But I don't know what the hell he's doing here. What are *you* doing here? What *is* all this?'

'Keep your shirt on.' His young self, placating, put his hand on Fergus's pyjama sleeve. 'Take it easy. You'll not get out of this by yelling like some stupid kid.'

'Out of what? Out of *what*?'

'Nothing. Just a figure of speech.'

'Hold on!' Fergus faced his younger face, saw the young eyes, shifty in the strange light of the full moon. 'Out of what? What am I in, what's happening to me?'

'Calm down,' his younger self said with a sudden yawn, which Fergus recognized as an old tic of his when he was nervous and afraid. 'Come on. They're waiting.'

'Who?'

'The family.'

'Look,' Fergus began, but his younger self signalled to him to be quiet. 'Please?' he said. 'Let's go.' And turned, beckoning Fergus to follow. Here, high on the beach, past the tide marks, the sand was powdery; their feet sank deep, making the walking slow. His young self peered ahead, tapping his pipe against his teeth.

'Stop that,' Fergus said. 'Get rid of the pipe; it makes you look silly.'

'What do you think *you* look like to *me*? Some middle-aged half-Yank, living with a girl my own age, working for films or something. Jesus, you're enough to make a person puke!'

Fergus laughed.

'You don't even lose your temper now! If anybody said that to me, I'd hit them.'

'Yes, I suppose you would.'

'You don't try to change anyone's opinions. You don't argue. You're somebody who'd avoid me, if you met me at a party. We wouldn't even get on.'

'Oh, I don't know about that,' Fergus said. 'I like you. I always did.'

His younger self bit his fingernail, a habit which made Fergus wince. Walking a few steps ahead of Fergus, he moved his shoulders uncomfortably in his ill-fitting jacket, swaying slightly as his feet sank in the floury sands. How pale he is, Fergus thought, how childish he looks. The bitten nails he had forgotten, but remembered the toes of the brown leather shoes, always badly scuffed, the cheap wristwatch, heavy and coarse, which he had once worn with such pride of ownership. And now the silly pipe was pocketed, and instead his young self produced a package of Woodbines, the same cheap cigarettes Paddy Donlon had used – coffin nails, people used to call them – and Fergus, who had been ordered by his doctor to give up cigarettes, stared with revulsion at this greedy young smoker, inhaling, opening his mouth to let the smoke drift up into his nostrils, a childish trick which made Fergus want to say something. But what use? This was his past. It had been done; it could not be undone. Instead, his young self, pointing up ahead, asked, 'Out there. The point? Where's that?'

'It's called Zuma Beach.'

'That's it, then,' his young self said. 'They're waiting for us there.'

'Who's waiting?'

'It's your birthday.'

'But my birthday's in August,' Fergus said. 'Remember? The whole family used to go to the seaside for a picnic.'

'Right. This is the strand, this year. Zuma Beach. That's the name Daddy said.'

'But it's the middle of the night!'

'It's not a normal situation,' his young self said. 'It's not even your birthday, by your reckoning.'

'And by yours?' Fergus asked. 'Is it different where you are?'

'Where I am?' his young self said. 'What do you mean?'

'I mean. You know. I mean, in the other world.'

'What other world?' asked his young self, slyly side-glancing Fergus, and kicking his toes in the powdery sand. 'Do you believe in another world?'

'You know I don't.'

'Well, then.'

They walked on in silence.

'Anyway,' said his younger self, pointing, 'I think that's them. Over there, by that log.'

Fergus turned up towards the dune, following his young self's lead, lagging behind a few steps as they approached a straggling circle of some twenty people who were sitting or kneeling in small groups in the sand, near the dead, grey trunk of a fallen tree. In the lee of the tree trunk, a white linen tablecloth already spread with food from opened wicker baskets, unbreakable picnic teacups and saucers laid out in a row, ready for tea and, fussing, pulling a piston in and out of a primus stove, Dr Fadden, kneeling, an old-fashionedly elegant holiday-maker in white Panama hat, the brim pulled rakishly down all around, brass-buttoned navy blazer, cream woollen flannels, white buck golf shoes with red-brick rubber soles, a cream tennis shirt with a striped silk foulard. And in a temper. 'Damn stove! Damn petrol's flooded the wick!'

Dr Fadden did not look up as Fergus approached, nor did any of the others who waited for the picnic. Fergus's mother and his Aunt Mary, both in summer dresses and wearing thirties hats, were busily arranging fruitcake, strawberries and cream, anchovy paste, macaroons, birthday cake, tongue slices, cream puffs, watercress sandwiches, egg salad, jam roll, ham sandwiches, strong mustard, salt, sugar, cream for the tea, all of it spreading like a great dark stain on the moonlit white cloth. Busy, silent, his mother and Aunt Mary ferried food from the picnic baskets to the tablecloth, working at great speed as though here, as so often in the past, the trick of the picnic was to get the food laid out, eaten, then packed away, before the inevitable Irish rain.

Fergus looked at his younger self, who had moved to the fringes of the group and now sat, his back to Fergus, pulling a car blanket about his shoulders as though he were suddenly cold. Unwelcomed, standing alone at this feast, which it was said, was being held in his honour, Fergus turned to look at the other picnickers, who, in a manner reminiscent of actors in some avant-garde stage production, sat in small groups, their heads averted, so that he, their audience, could not see who they were. Waiting, as though their turn had not yet come, they, like those manipulators of puppets in Japanese theatre, seemed part of a convention, invisible because they so willed it. Thus his attention was forced back to the one recognizable group highlighted by brilliant moonlight, performing as on a stage – his father, fussing with the primus stove, and in the background, his mother and Aunt Mary laying out the food. He went towards them.

'Hello, Daddy.'

'You're late,' his father said, not looking up, still twisting and pumping the primus stove.

'Late?'

'We've come all this way, made all these arrangements, the least you could do is be on time.'

'But how was I to know?' Fergus heard himself complain in the aggrieved tone he had used as a child when his father accused him unjustly of wrong-doing.

'All right, all right,' Dr Fadden said. 'That's enough. Let's not lose our tempers. We've got a number of people here who want to meet you. This is supposed to be a happy occasion, I believe.'

'Is it? I'm glad to hear it. I was beginning to get the impression that I'd done something wrong. That I was on trial or something.'

'Trial?' Dr Fadden fitted his pince-nez spectacles to the bridge of his nose and looked through them at Fergus. 'What are you talking about, sir?'

'I'm not sure. But, this afternoon, in the living room, those people seemed to be judging me.'

'In the living room?' Dr Fadden shook his head, amused. 'I never heard of a court of law in a living room, did you?'

'No, but then, I never heard of a picnic in the middle of the night.'

'Picnic? This is no picnic, believe you me!'

'What is it then, Daddy?'

'What am I?' said his father irritably. 'Some sort of question box? Off you go! All these people are here on your behalf. The least you can do is mingle. Mix, boy, mix!'

His father, producing his bullet-shaped lighter, flamed it and flamed the primus. 'Kettle, dear!' he called in his operating-theatre manner, and at once Fergus's mother hurried up with a special light aluminium picnic kettle. As she passed Fergus, she turned her head and said, 'You heard your father. Go on!'

Fergus, obedient from habit, turned from the tea-making tableau and walked past the spread tablecloth towards a group of three figures who sat, their backs to him, their knees hunched up, staring at the breaking, phosphorescence-tinged waves. Coming up behind them, noticing that all three were women and that, sitting side by side, they were: Sophie Lavery, the first girl he had imagined himself in love with, but, in effect, had never managed to date, and had kissed only once, during a party game. Eileen Roche, the first girl who allowed him to make love to her (now remembered only vaguely as a wild, bad-tempered creature he had known for three weeks on a Youth Hostel holiday). He was eighteen at the time and she twenty-three, she said. At the end of the line was Margaret, the woman who was still his legal wife, her fox's mask cross and furtive, as, sighting him, she leaned close to the other two and whispered of his presence. He stood, looked at the three faces lit by moonlight, as, malicious, his wife drew the other two women's heads close, punctuating whatever it was she was saying by a series of sniggers. Sophie Lavery, the girl he had worshipped from a distance, seemed surprised at what was being told her, but bad-tempered Eileen Roche was clearly irritated by his wife's nervous habit of digging at her listeners with her elbow. He looked again at the woman he had once married, a gossip, a self-dramatizer, and in the Irish saying, 'at present a praiser of her own past'. Three women, three faces. He could think of nothing he might say to them. His former wife, whispering, sniggered again in a delight of self-amusement. He walked on.

On the edge of the picnic area was a steep sand dune. Down the dune, rolling over and over like a corpse down a trench, came Lise. He waited until, all momentum expended, she lay prone and motionless on level sands. Then walked towards her and stood, looking down at her.

'Hi,' he said.

'Oh, hello, Dad.'

'Was that fun?'

'Sort of.'

'Good.'

Embarrassment was now the only emotion they shared. Indifference would, he suspected, be the next progression. He feared that. He did not know what Lise feared; perhaps their meetings.

'Ungk-wungk!' Lise said, and shutting her small fists, beat them against her flat, pre-pubescent chest. He laughed gratefully. The gorilla in the Central Park Zoo had said 'Ungk-wungk!' and beat its blue leather chest. On their Sundays together they had often gone to the zoo.

'How's school this year?'

'Okay, I guess.'

She did not ask him what he was doing on this beach in the middle of the night. He did not explain why he had not been to see her in six months. This was not the real Lise. The real Lise had refused to come and visit him in California. This Lise sat up, clutching her knees, and looked at the breaking waves. 'It's funny,' she said, 'you hardly ever see animals on the beach. Except dogs. And birds, I guess, but they don't count.'

'I remember,' he said, 'when I was a kid in Ireland, on the beaches there, you sometimes saw cows, just walking along, right down by the waves.'

He saw the cows as he said it, aimless clumps of cows, ambling along the strand in Kerry.

'But why cows?' Lise asked.

'Why not?'

'What would cows do on a beach?'

'I don't know.'

'I mean, would they come to eat grass? Or swim?'

'They just used to walk.'

'Oh,' she said. He felt she did not believe him. It was always a mistake to say 'when I was a kid'. Children were uncomprehending that grown-ups could ever have been like them. His love for his daughter was like the love affairs of his adolescence. He loved Lise but had no notion of what she really wanted. And so, his contacts with her depended on a mutual, heightened mood, difficult to sustain, easily deflected into irritations and tedium.

'Is there ice cream?' Lise asked.

'What?'

'At this picnic?'

'I suppose so,' he said. 'Go over there. Ask my mother.'

'Daddy!' Lise stood up, amused, brushing sand from her skirt. 'You mean *my* mother, don't you? She's over there with those two girls.'

'No. *My* mother. Your grandmother. Come on, I'll introduce you.'

'Oh, stop it,' Lise said, irritated with him. 'It's not fair calling Mummy a grandmother. You're always awfully mean to her.'

'Wait now, you don't get it,' he said, too late, for Lise, angry, jumped up and said, 'I have to go,' and ran across the sands. Back to that new life with Mummy and Mummy's good friends, a new life which was his unregretted past, now dissolved in a sour aftertaste, its only legacy this only child. And yet, he remembered, it is not the real Lise who is running away from me now, only my memory of Lise. I no longer know today's Lise, and in a few years, the girl I meet again will not be that ten-year-old who was once my only daughter.

'Propagation of the Faithful,' said a mocker's voice, and behind him he heard sudden, hard, male laughter. He swung around alarmed, although he did not know why, and there were men beginning to form a circle, surrounding him on the sands, men whose faces he could not quite distinguish. A cloud seemed to have darkened the moonlight which had lit the beach, and the

143

men, laughing softly, whispering to each other, kept moving, dodging like agitators taking part in a public demonstration, avoiding his policeman's eye. 'Yes, the Catholic aim in life is the propagation of the faithful,' the mocker said again. 'That was one of your man Fergus's so-called *bons mots*.'

'Aye,' said another voice. 'Fergus Fadden, the La Roche-foucauld of the Antrim Road.'

That was Hugh Gildea, the poet: it sounded just like him. 'Gildea?' Fergus called. 'Is that you, Gildea?'

But whoever it was dodged back in the darkness, while the others, laughing, whispering, set up a confused static of voices, electric, minatory, the courtroom buzz he had heard that afternoon. Moving around him, circling, whispering to each other in head-turning asides. Now he began to see their faces. They were not faces he could put a name to, but they were familiar – the faces of old men and young men. Some might be American, some might be English or Irish; most had no clearly defined nationality, and yet, in each instance as he stared at the men's features, a name came into his throat, but like a failed connection, died before it reached shape in his brain. Circling, whispering, grouped as though to detain him, perhaps to harm him, the men jostled against each other, and from time to time laughed softly, as at some private, unpleasant joke.

'Wait,' he said, stretching out his arm to point to a fair-haired youth now passing close to him. 'Wait, don't I know you, I just can't recall, but I seem to remember, we were friends, I'm sure? What's your name? Give me a clue?'

'Give me a clue?' the youth repeated mockingly in a soft southern Irish brogue. The others laughed, moving, circling Fergus, their whispered words coming to him in a jumble.

'Remember?'

'Says he doesn't –'

'Of course he does –'

'Give him a clue?'

'Name? Wants my name? Did you hear him?'

'Pretending –'

'Of course, he's –'

'He remembers –'

'Of course – sure he does –'

'Remembers –'

Then all laughed in unison, a quick surge of amusement, as at the tag line of a joke. 'But, listen,' Fergus called, feeling himself dry-mouthed, and beginning to stammer. 'Wait, I'm not kidding. I don't remember, I'm not pretending, my memory . . . it's, it's been a long time! If you'd just stand still a minute, stop moving around, let me look at you. The light is bad. It's clouded over.'

They laughed.

'Wants us to stop the clock,' an American voice said. 'That's what he wants.'

An old voice grumbled. 'Men don't stop time. Time stops men.'

They laughed again, and then, abrupt, as though obeying some covert command, all froze to attention and stood, their heads turning in an eyes-right gesture. Fergus, following the direction of their gaze, saw the other picnickers, those silent figures who had sat anonymous in shadow, now rise and begin to walk towards the circle. The moon, which had been moving behind rags of cloud, shone bright again as the circle parted to admit a girl, who walked up to Fergus, a girl whose face was not familiar to him, young, but hard to put an age to, the colour of whose hair and eyes he could not quite make out, a pretty girl, but not one to make men's heads turn. 'Fergus?' she said, and stood, meek yet confident of recognition. 'How are you, Fergus?'

'Fine,' he said. 'I'm fine.' Who was she?

'You've not changed,' she said.

'No?'

'No. And me, have I changed?'

'I suppose,' he said uncertainly. 'Yes, I suppose you must have.'

He was being watched. Not only the men who formed the circle, but the newcomers, arriving, shifted and craned to see, as though he and the girl were itinerant performers at some country fair.

'In what way have I changed, Fergus?'

'What was that?' he asked. A wrong answer, he felt, might provoke the crowd to turn on him.

'I said, in what way have I changed?'

'I don't know. Maybe it's, ah, maybe it's just the moonlight?'

'You've seen me in the moonlight before.'

Some of the onlookers laughed.

'Well, perhaps it's your hair?' he said. That should be safe. Women were always changing their hair styles.

'Oh? Had I cut it by the time I met you? I suppose I had. No, it must have been later. It was Tom's idea that I cut it. Don't you remember?'

Fergus shook his head. *Tom?*

'You remember what he's like once he decides on something. Remember that thing he was always saying to you, you know, about, "When a thing's worth doing, it's really worth doing." '

'If a thing's worth doing, it's worth doing well,' Fergus corrected her. He still had no idea who Tom was. That was something his mother used to say.

'Worth doing well!' the girl said. 'Yes, that's exactly it. So you do remember, after all. You know, for a moment there, I thought you *had* forgotten us. I know that's not possible, you couldn't really have such a poor memory, but still . . .'

Someone in the circle of watchers began to cough, a harsh, uncontrollable cough. 'Shhhh!' several voices warned the cougher.

'We tried to see you when we came to New York,' the girl said. 'But I suppose you were away at the time. I wrote you a letter, then a postcard, and when we got to New York, we phoned your number two or three times. But there was never any answer.'

'He was dodging you,' a raucous Ulster voice called from the crowd. 'He didn't want to see you!'

Fergus, looking past the girl at the spectators, caught sight of his father and mother on the fringe of the circle. Both were peering about uneasily to see who had spoken against their son. Fergus, catching his mother's eye, smiled at her, but his mother, although she stared right at him, did not acknowledge his smile of recognition any more than she would have reacted to the smile of an actor onstage.

'No,' the girl said. 'I admit that the thought crossed my mind. But Tom said no, Tom said you'd never ignore an old friend.'

'Old friend! That's a good one,' the Ulster voice yelled, and

146

this time, turning quickly, Fergus saw the heckler. It was Niall Nelligan, Kathleen's husband, whom Fergus always thought of as the brother-in-law. The brother-in-law had never liked him.

'Old friend,' the brother-in-law shouted again. 'Sure, he's like all these bloody journalists and novelists, going in among ordinary, decent people, then coming away and writing filthy, dirty, disgusting lies about them. Just like I'm sure he did about you.'

'Oh, no,' the girl said. 'I don't think he ever wrote anything about what happened. He gave up journalism shortly after we knew him. And he didn't write about us in either of his novels, did you, Fergus?'

'Not that I know of,' said Fergus truthfully. Who was she? Who was Tom? The crowd edged closer. The circle, thickened by newcomers arriving on its outer edges, pressed in on him and on the girl. There were many, many more people than he had first imagined.

'Sheila's twelve now,' the girl said. 'She's very curious about you. You're her godfather, remember?'

'Oh?' he said. Godfather? He was godfather to two children that he knew of, his nephew and John Dowling's girl, whose name was Denise.

'He doesn't remember,' yelled the brother-in-law. 'He dropped you, forgot all about you. You weren't important enough!'

'No, no,' the unknown girl said. 'That's not fair. Fergus isn't like that. I'll never forget those times, and I'm sure you won't either, will you Fergus?'

The last newspaper Fergus had worked for was the *Long Island Gazette*, a weekly he had edited in the Hamptons. From what this girl said, he had known her and the mysterious Tom at that time. What year was that? But here, in the moonlight, surrounded by these vaguely hostile figures from his former life, his mind, panicked, could not function: no memory came of those times, of these names, of this girl now staring in his face.

'No,' said a voice. 'He will not forget.'

Into the circle, a strange black-skirted figure in the moonlight, stepped Father Alonzo Aloysius Allen, a Passionist Father from Mount Muckish Monastery, County Donegal, known as the greatest mission preacher in Ireland. On his head, the cruciform

147

shape of a biretta, its pompom adornment giving his harsh, pinched face the caricature aspect of an angry Punchinello. His black serge soutane, its breast emblazoned with the black-and-white Sacred Heart and Cross badge of the Passionist Order, was adorned also by a short shoulder cape, peaked back dandyishly to reveal an underlining of red silk. The crowd, suddenly respectful, turned towards the voice of sacerdotal authority.

'No,' said Father Alonzo Allen. 'He will not forget. He will not forget, because he cannot forget. If I forget thee, O Jerusalem, may my right hand be forgotten. He cannot forget, as Adam and Eve could not forget, as the great saint, Augustine, Bishop of Hippo, could not forget, as we, each and every one of us, cannot, must not, will not forget that we have sinned, we have sinned against the light, we are the children of wrath, miserable weaklings each and every one of us, we have sinned, and those sins cannot be wiped out, they have stained the soul, and that stain must be washed clean in the flames of purgatory, leaving only a bitter memory, a memory which will never desert us, a knowledge that we have sinned against our Lord Jesus Christ, and now, to take it down to the particular, right down to the *ad hominem*, so to speak, to this soul in front of us tonight, Fergus Patrick Fadden, son of good Catholic parents, born into a family strong in the true faith, a boy who had every advantage of good Catholic schools, of religious instruction, of Christian precept and example, yes, every advantage, every opportunity, and what has become of this boy, I ask you, what has become of him? Yes, I say to him, I say in the words of our Blessed Lord Himself: "It is impossible that scandals should not come, but woe to him through whom they come. It were better for him that a millstone be tied around his neck and cast into the sea than that he should scandalize one of these little ones." Those are the words of our blessed Saviour, words which might have been addressed to this very man before you, this defiler of young girls, this adulterer, fornicator, scandal-giver, a very anti-Christ of iniquity, a moral cesspool, but – and I say *but* – if any man or woman here tonight believes that this foul sinner standing here before us has sunk so low in the stinking stew of his vices that he has forgotten one single sinful thought, word, or deed that he has committed, then you had better think again, my good people, for I say to you to-night, man, born of woman, man, born into this vale of tears, man, marked by that first sin committed by the woman Eve in the garden of Eden, that original sin that cannot be wiped out, that sin which mankind cannot forget, because Almighty God will not allow mankind to forget, I say to you that this man, Fergus Fadden, standing before you on this strand tonight, is – may the Lord have mercy on his soul! – a liar! Yes, a prevaricator, an obfuscator, a bearer of false witness, a serpentine, sly, sibilant snake, sliding down the slimy paths of untruth. A liar, yes, a liar, I say, who is trying to conceal from this poor girl, and from you, good people, the simple, plain, straight truth of this matter, which is that he does not forget, not at all! And why is he trying to conceal the truth, why is he pretending to you, and God forgive him, maybe even pretending to his own self, that he cannot remember this poor girl? Well, I put it to you! I ask each and every one of you here tonight to look into his or her heart, to examine your consciences this minute and ask yourselves one question. One question! What conclusions do you draw from this man's behaviour tonight? Think! What conclusion *must* you draw!'

'Good man, yourself, Father!'

'Aye, that's telling him!'

'A great preacher, a great priest of God!'

'God bless you and keep you, Father Allen!'

'Say a prayer for me, Father!'

'Yes, remember us in your nightly devotions, Father Alonzo!'

'A saint, that priest is, a saint of God!'

Father Alonzo Aloysius Allen, tossing back the peaks of his shoulder, raised his hands, palms out to the crowd, stilling the cries and the applause. 'Do your Christian duty,' he intoned. 'And may the Lord forgive him, and forgive us all. Amen!'

So saying, raising his biretta in acknowledgement of the crowd's applause, Father Allen moved into the crowd as though hurrying to keep an appointment. The spectators parted respectfully to let him pass, then reformed, freshly aroused, around Fergus and the unknown girl.

'Conor?' someone called. 'Is Conor Findlater here?'

'Yes, come on, Lugs. Come on up here.'

'Right then, lads,' said the dentist, Lugs Findlater himself, shouldering his way to the front of the crowd, stepping into the ring with Fergus, showing a clenched fist the size of a small cauliflower. 'What happened? Were you spying on this girl's naked body the way you spied on my wife? You bloody hoor's get, I've a good mind to knock your flaming head off.'

'Yes, what happened, what happened, tell us?' called out an old woman dressed in black, whom Fergus recognized as Mrs Jacky Kelly, his mother's charlady and a powerful gossip. 'Give us the juicy bits, Master Fergus! Go on! Sure and I'll not tell nobody.'

'The juicy bits!' several voices repeated, and at the rear of the crowd, a newspaper poster was elevated for Fergus to see. It read:

The News of the World
All Human Life Is There.

The unknown girl, studying the newspaper poster, turned and caught Fergus's sleeve. 'What do they mean? What are they talking about?'

'I don't know.'

A hand gripped his pyjama collar, and he was spun around to face Dr Terry MacMahon, F.R.C.S., D.O.M., who had fitted him for glasses when he was a child. In Dr MacMahon's hand was a pencil flashlight, which he shone into Fergus's right pupil. 'Amnesia will get you nowhere,' Dr MacMahon said absently. 'Now, look me in the eye. Hmm! What did you do to this girl?'

'Nothing. On my word of honour.'

'How can you give your word of honour when you can't even read that chart?' Dr MacMahon asked. 'The whole thing's a blur to you, isn't it?'

'Well, yes.'

'He took her knickers down,' Old Mrs Jacky Kelly told the others. 'Yes, he took down her knicky-knacks, then opened up he's flies and tried to force he's will on her in an immoral action.'

'I did not.' Trembling, Fergus tried to look past the bright light of Dr MacMahon's pencil flashlight; but the moonlit circle of faces remained blurred and distant.

'The dirrty baste!' a Kerry voice thundered. 'Showing his naked member to an innocent girl. Desperate carry-on! What else did he do, Missis Kelly? Give us all the dirt.'

'Aye, that's what he done, right enough,' Mrs Jacky Kelly said, nodding portentously. 'Exposed he's private parts to her. Then threatened her wi' he's fists. Threw her down and had he's will of her. Then run off to America, leaving her in the fambly way.'

'Nonsense!' Fergus heard himself shout. 'I'd never do a thing like that, and if there was anything even remotely like it, I'd certainly not forget it!'

'Why, you can't see the nose in front of your face,' Dr Mac-Mahon said sternly. 'Here, try this.'

A pair of steel optical test frames were clamped onto Fergus's nose. The doctor selected a lens from a wooden box and slid the lens into the right eye socket of the frames. 'Shut the other eye. Now, how's that?'

Beyond the doctor's hand, the blurry frieze of faces became clear, hard-edged. Hostile faces. 'Look,' Fergus said. 'Let me try to explain? Most people live their lives in one place, and they meet, essentially, the same people, year after year. But I've lived in Ireland, worked as a newspaperman in England and France, came to America and worked on Long Island, then in New York, and now I'm here on the Pacific. I'm trying to say I've lived in so many places, it's impossible to remember –'

'Prevaricator! Obfuscator!' thundered the voice of Father Alonzo Aloysius Allen.

'No, it's true! I really *don't* remember this lady, though she obviously remembers me, and I'm very sorry about that, for her sake. I know how hurtful it can be if people don't remember who you are.'

'Bloody fraud!' shouted the voice of the brother-in-law.

'No, please, I'm trying to explain, when I look around at you, there are so many of you, there are faces I don't recognize right away –'

'All right, then try this,' Dr MacMahon interrupted, sliding a new lens into the optical frame. The frieze of faces blurred to a milky jumble.

'I mean,' Fergus said, 'I mean, I know I must remember all of you, otherwise you wouldn't be here, but even though I can't place each one of you, you're all somewhere inside my head. If you'll only give me time, help me – I mean –' He turned to the unknown girl. 'If *you* could give me your name? Or a place? Some clue?'

The dentist elbowed the girl aside and faced Fergus. 'You know who *I* am, don't you, laddie? Too bloody right you do. And who's this?'

The dentist turned, and taking the hand of a little girl, led her into the centre of the circle. The child was about twelve. 'Well?' asked the dentist.

'I'm sorry, I don't know.'

'This is your goddaughter,' the dentist said. 'This woman's child. Or it could be she's more to you than your goddaughter, knowing the way *you* work.'

Laughter, like a coughing fit, shook and ruffled the body of the crowd. The unknown woman turned to face her tormentors. 'That's a terrible thing to say,' she began in a high, tearful voice. 'This is *my* daughter. Our daughter. Tom's and mine. And it's true that Fergus is her godfather, but it's not fair to ask him to recognize her. He left for New York before she was born.'

'There's many's a one put on he's hat and went down the road and never was heard of again,' old Mrs Jacky Kelly whispered to her neighbours. 'There's many's the boy crossed the water to England or America to get out of crossing the church door.'

'I'm an ophthalmic surgeon,' Dr MacMahon told the crowd. 'But I can, if necessary, recommend the proper man for this job. Tricky, though, this business of establishing who's the child's real father.'

'Aye, too right it is,' the dentist said, thrusting Fergus's goddaughter back into the ranks of the bystanders. 'Especially since some of these English dollies would open their legs to anything in pants.'

The unknown girl, distraught, caught at Fergus's sleeve. 'Why do they say things like that?'

'Because they're Irish,' Fergus said. 'A nation of masturbators under priestly instruction.'

'All right, now, that will do,' said Dr MacMahon, plucking the steel optical frames from Fergus's nose. 'You have a case of myopia. Unable to take the long view.'

Father Alonzo Allen, kicking the skirts of his soutane, like a bride trying to manage a difficult train, passed ominously through the crowd, intoning, 'None so blind as those who will not see. The Irish people know that it is not this world that counts. This life is but a preparation for eternity. Guard against sin, especially those sins of the flesh which degrade us in the sight of God and of His Holy Mother!'

'Amen,' said several of the spectators. Some made the Sign of the Cross, and others, sensing a commotion, turned towards the outer fringes of the crowd as way was made for Fergus's mother, who, stout, pregnant, wearing a big-brimmed garden-party hat with a mauve ribbon, and a pale grey crêpe-de-chine summer dress in the style of the late nineteen-thirties, came through the ranks to the inner rim of the circle, holding in front of her a white, iced birthday cake, decorated with walnuts and lit by eight red candles. 'Now, Fergus,' said she, stopping in front of him, holding the cake up for his inspection and approval. The candles guttered in the wind as Dr MacMahon, gentlemanly, removed his grey felt hat and held it sideways, shielding the flames. The crowd was silent, almost reverent, as Fergus, uncertain as to what was expected of him, turned to face his mother and her gift. 'Now,' said his mother, 'you must make a wish. Then, if you blow out all the candles with one breath, your wish will come true.'

They were waiting; everyone was watching him; he must think of a wish before the candles went out in the wind. If only he could remember what it was he most wanted to wish for? 'I wish,' he said, 'I wish I could remember what it is I want to wish for. I wish I – yes, that's it, I wish I could remember! I mean, I often feel that I've done something wrong, made an enemy of someone, or made a fool of myself, but I can't be sure what it was I said or did. If I had total recall, then I wouldn't go on making the same mistakes, year after year. Yes, that's it. I want to remember. The big things, the small things, all the things I keep forgetting I've done or should do. That's my wish.'

'Tch, tch, tch,' his mother said. 'How often have I told you, you mustn't tell anyone your wish. You must make it in secret. Telling it spoils it.'

'Ah, now, Julia, have a heart!' His Aunt Mary hurried forward, and as she had when he was a child, swept Fergus into her arms, pressing his face against her old, musty, black bosom. 'Your mother is quite right, of course,' Aunt Mary said. 'A wish should be secret. But, you know, with the sea so loud behind us, I don't believe any of us heard what you said. Did we?' She turned, appealing to the onlookers, but unwilling to aid her conspiracy, their collective gaze remained fixed on the lighted candles and the cake. 'All right, son,' Aunt Mary said. 'Give a good big blow now.'

His mother elevated the cake as though holding up a chalice for adoration. Fergus eyed the eight candles, then closed his eyes and blew, ballooning his cheeks, puffing with all his wind. The crowd uttered an 'Ah!' of pleasure or disappointment. He opened his eyes and with a ridiculous wrench of dismay saw that he had failed to blow out all the candles. Two still flickered in reproach. He shifted position and blew again. Both flames were extinguished, but he felt only the most minor sense of accomplishment. The crowd began a half-hearted round of hand-clapping. A few people raised a cheer.

'That's the good boy,' Aunt Mary said. She winked at him, his old conspirator. '*I* baked that birthday cake,' she whispered. 'It's almond sponge inside. That's your favourite, isn't it?'

But Fergus's mother, overhearing this, shook her head in disapproval. 'No, Mary. When they've done wrong, they have to be punished. You have to tell them the truth, Fergus.'

'Yes, Mama.'

'You know what I'm talking about, don't you, Fergus?'

'You're saying I won't get my wish.'

'I didn't say you will, and I didn't say you won't. I'm just telling you the rules,' his mother said, turning, handing the birthday cake to Maeve. 'We'll need a bread knife to cut this cake.'

'Don't you stir,' Aunt Mary said. 'I'll get it.'

'Are we going to put it on plates and pass it around?' Maeve asked.

'Yes,' said his mother. 'You come with us, then, Mary. The plates are up there with the other picnic stuff.'

Aunt Mary nodded agreement. The three women made their way among the onlookers, going out of the circle and up the sands, first Maeve, carrying the cake, then his mother, then Aunt Mary, walking towards the sand dunes where the Primus stove burned bright in the moonlight, boiling the kettle for tea, where the wicker hampers stood, their lids open, the white linen cloth, weighted at its corners by stones, the fruitcake, strawberries and cream, anchovy paste, macaroons, tongue slices, cream puffs, watercress sandwiches, egg salad, jam roll, ham sandwiches, all ready for the eating. He wanted to be there, to go back to those birthday picnics where, after everyone had swum, or paddled in the sea, or walked on the sands, or hunted in rock pools, there would be this summer feast, and afterwards the birthday cake would be cut up and tasted, and he would be given his birthday presents to open, there on the strand, the envy of his brothers and sisters, the birthday boy, unscoldable, to whom, on that one day of the year, all would be allowed.

But this was not day, it was night; it was not Portstewart strand in Ireland, but Zuma Beach in southern California. It was not his birthday; nothing would be forgiven him. The crowd, closing ranks when the three women had made their way out to the picnic ground, shifted in mood, as though some Unholy Ghost in the biblical form of tongues of fire had come down from the night sky to settle in their bodies. No longer a grouping of individual onlookers, they were now, ineluctably, one – that violent, restless, head-strong creature, a mob.

'He shouldn't be allowed to get away with it!'

'Needs to be taught a lesson!'

He did not see the speakers who uttered these threats, and in the bank of faces at which he stared, no head turned at this sound of angry shouts. Rather, the mob, as though hearing its inner voice, muttered and rumbled as, inching closer, it narrowed the circumference of the circle surrounding Fergus and the unknown girl.

'Wait!' Fergus heard his own voice, high, uncertain, the voice of a victim, edged with panic. 'Now, look.' He stepped forward, holding up his hand as though to detain them. 'I want to co-operate, I want to get to the bottom of this, I want to do whatever is right. I'm here to be of any assistance. Solving this mystery is in my interest, every bit as much as it is in yours. Believe me, I'm completely at your service.'

'What mystery, laddie?' called a harsh voice, the voice which had rendered judgement on him that afternoon. 'What mystery? All you're trying to do is conceal the true facts.'

'What facts? Who said that?' Fergus cried. 'Who's accusing me? And what are you accusing me of?'

Someone punched him on the shoulder. Someone else punched him from behind, striking a blow at the base of his skull. He could not see who had struck him, and when he turned to the girl beside him, she also had been attacked. There was an ugly cut on her cheek, and someone had ripped off her skirt, revealing her, pathetic, in an unattractive green-flowered panty girdle.

'You leave her alone!' Fergus shouted shakily, staring at the hostile blur of faces.

'Did you?' a male voice called.

'I told you. I don't remember. If anything had happened, if there was ever anything between us, of course I'd remember!'

'Do you remember me?' A woman thrust herself forward to confront him. She was very pretty and had strange eyes, bright blue irises, flecked with brown. He did not know her.

'We met at the Carters' apartment in New York. You sat down and spent the entire evening talking to me. After a while, people began to notice. Your wife was irritated and made ugly little jokes, but you ignored her. Then we met, by chance, later that summer, on the beach at Westhampton. We went for a walk in the dunes, and you hurried me on ahead of the others. You said you'd thought of me every single day. I believed you. I had often thought of you. You said if only we'd met five years earlier, if only we weren't both married to other people. You said you would never forget me. You said you would always think of me. There were tears in your eyes. You kissed me when we said good-bye.'

'Mrs Vakalo,' Fergus said. 'Erica Vakalo! I meant it.'

'But, look,' the woman said. 'I'm me as I was at the time you met me. Yet you seemed puzzled when you saw me just now. And all those years, sometimes when I'd feel depressed about growing old, I'd think of you and think that there you were, somewhere, remembering me as I was. I thought of you as the person who will always think of me. But you weren't thinking of me at all.'

Erica Vakalo turned away. A boy ran forward, a boy in short grey flannel trousers, school tie, grey flannel shirt. 'Fergus?' he called.

'You're someone from St Michan's,' Fergus said, staring at him nervously.

'You're joking,' the boy said, and turned, grinning at the crowd. 'Fergus is a great joker,' the boy said.

'He's not joking. He forgot you,' a voice called. The crowd, in unison, mumbled angry agreement.

'He wouldn't, no,' the boy said. 'We're best friends, we swore we'd always be. Listen, we went every place together, we shared, we went halfers on sweets and toys and everything. He held my coat if I had to fight anybody, and I held his when it was his turn.'

'Ownie!' Fergus said. 'Ownie Dempster!'

'There!' the boy said triumphantly, grinning at the crowd. 'I told you he wouldn't forget.'

'He didn't know you from Adam. You gave it away!'

'No, I didn't!' the boy said.

'You did! He'd have passed you by in the street.'

It's true, I would, Fergus thought, staring at the boy, who, his grin failing him, turned this way and that, searching for the unseen heckler, little Ownie Dempster, loyal Ownie, who had been beaten up in the cloister walk at St Michan's by Turkington's gang because he was Fergus Fadden's friend. *Ownie*. They had always been together in those years, he and Ownie. Yet he had not thought of him since; did not even know where Ownie was, or what had become of him. Was he a doctor now, a priest, or what?

Silent, eyes staring, movingly restlessly around Fergus and the girl, the mob seemed to await some violent command. If only he could guess what it wanted, what words from him would forestall

157

this mad group rage. But as he studied the faces, he felt more confused, more apprehensive. His mind, bereft of memory, remained blank, and now there was no face he knew here; he looked for Father Alonzo Allen. Perhaps *he* was the heckler? But the priests he saw peering from the outer fringes of the crowd were all strangers. He looked for his brother Jim and saw two boys, either one of whom might be Jim; he could not be sure. He turned right and left, searching for some half-familiar face, panic filling his mouth as he realized that this might be the moment when his memory, contrary, unbiddable, deserted him forever, and now, as though confirming his fear, men, women, boys, girls, began to step out from the ranks, one by one, like soldiers on a parade ground, each staring directly into his face, then stepping back, while, all the while, the crowd seemed to chant (but he could not be sure whether he heard or only seemed to hear) one word, over and over, menacing, questioning: 'Remember? Remember? Remember?' the staring faces accusatory, as, deafened by the chant and dazed by the faces thrust in front of him, then withdrawn, he felt several unseen assailants pummel him in the back of his neck, in his kidneys, in his groin. 'Remember? Remember? Remember?' Beaten, he fell to his knees, stumbling like a camel going down in the sands as the chant changed, and he heard the angry voices call: 'You forgot, you forgot, you forgot!'

Panting, sickened, his head bowed, he found himself staring at the toecaps of the shoes of the mob, sensing beside him the presence of the unknown girl, her hair falling over her bleeding face, her clothing torn, her breathing painful, hurt, and suddenly the outrage of this – this stranger being made to suffer for him – broke into his panic, and he rose up, shouting: 'Wait! Stop!' And saw the mob, caught in that one moment of his resistance, go slack, and uncertain, its fury checked.

'Where is my father?' Fergus heard himself ask, and the crowd, uneasy, broke ranks, parting in a broad lane through which he walked as though in a trance, still floating in panic, for what if he did not recognize even his own father, what if he were truly lost, his memory dead, mindless, without a past – what? But as he walked on, the crowd drawing back to let him pass, he saw at the far end of the lane an opening where, away from the mob, a small group sat, the picnic group he had first come upon when he reached this part of the beach. His father (he could have wept with the relief of knowing it was his father), cross-legged, in navy blazer, cream flannels, white buck shoes; his mother, Aunt Mary, Maeve, Jim, Kathleen, all around the picnic cloth, its soiled plates, empty teacups, disarranged cakes, evidence that the picnic itself had already been eaten. Jim was ten years old. Maeve wore her school uniform, Kathleen was seventeen. All looked up at him; they had been waiting.

'All right,' his father said. 'We're ready. Fire away.'

'What do you mean?'

'Fergus?' Aunt Mary whispered. He turned to look at her. 'Animal, vegetable, or mineral?' Aunt Mary whispered. 'That's the first thing you ask.'

'My God,' Fergus said. 'Twenty Questions!'

'Of course it's Twenty Questions,' his father said. 'We've played it thousands of times. What's the matter with you?'

'Come along, Fergus,' his mother said. 'You want to find out what it is, don't you?'

'But this isn't a game!' Fergus shouted. 'Those people back there were beating me. They want to kill me. And that poor girl, they damn near tore her clothes off! If I hadn't remembered to ask for you, Daddy, God knows what would have happened!'

'Well, then,' his father said. 'Let's get on with it. What is it you want to know?'

'What does that mob want of me? Who's that girl? What am I supposed to have done?'

'Fergus,' his father said patiently, 'you have twenty questions.'

They would not change; they would do it their way or not at all. 'Is it animal?' Fergus asked.

'Yes, it is,' Aunt Mary told him. 'There you are. You see, you've made a grand start.'

'Animal.' Fergus said. 'Is it someone who's here now?'

'Well . . .' Maeve seemed doubtful. 'It could be.'

'That's not an answer, Maeve,' his father said. 'We must answer yes or no.'

'Let's say yes,' Fergus's mother said. 'Yes, Fergus.'

'Is it a member of the family, then?' Fergus asked.

'No!' Jim, gleeful, hitched up his long wool socks.

'Is it someone in that crowd back there?'

'Yes,' said Dr Fadden.

'Is it something I should know about them?'

'Yes.'

'So,' said Fergus. 'It's animal, it's someone in that crowd back there, and it's something I should know about them. Is this person male or female?'

'That's not a proper question,' Jim said. 'We can't answer yes or no to it.'

'Is this person male?'

'No.'

'Is this person female?'

'Hah!' said Jim, pleased. 'You didn't have to ask that. If a person isn't male, they have to be female, don't they? That's seven questions. You have thirteen left.'

'If it's a female in that crowd back there and it's something I should know about them, then I suppose it's that girl who says I'm the godfather of her child?'

'Yes!' Aunt Mary said. 'Very good. You're getting warm.'

'Is it the girl's name? Is that the thing I should remember?'

'No,' said Maeve.

'Ten questions left,' Jim said.

'Is it connected with her husband?'

'Well . . . yes.'

'Was it something to do with the godchild?'

'No.'

'Is it something I did to her?'

There was a pause. The family looked to Dr Fadden for a ruling. 'No-o,' said Dr Fadden in a voice which made Fergus sure he was getting close to the answer.

'Is it something I did *with* her, then?'

'Well . . . yes.'

'Was it a pleasant action?'

'Yes,' said Aunt Mary.

'Did it hurt her, later?'

'No,' said Dr Fadden.

'So it was something I did in connection with that girl which did not hurt her and which was pleasant. Was it pleasant for both of us?'

'Yes,' said his mother.

'Did it displease anyone else?'

'No,' said his father.

'Then it wasn't something I should be ashamed of, was it?'

'No.'

'Did it help her, was it something which helped her?'

'Yes.'

'Was it financial? Did I help her financially?'

'Too late!' Jim cried triumphantly. 'Twenty Questions!'

'So it *was* financial,' Fergus said. 'That's the answer, isn't it?'

'No, dear,' said Aunt Mary. 'But you came very close.'

'Listen to me, all of you!' Fergus said. 'The game is over. But that mob back there thinks something reprehensible happened between me and that girl. And because I can't remember who she is, I can't defend myself. Don't you see? Forgetting is the most terrible thing that can happen to a person. You must help me. It's your duty!'

'Duty?' his father said. 'Why duty?'

'Aren't we here on earth to help each other? Isn't that what you always told me?'

Dr Fadden shook his head. 'We are here on earth for one reason, and for one reason only. To save our immortal souls.' Calm, he produced a yellow package of Wills Gold Flake cigarettes, extracted a cigarette, and lit it with his bullet-shaped lighter. Below, on the beach, the mob had reformed and was now coming up the strand, like some disorderly procession, moving in angry mass towards the picnic site.

'Your Twenty Questions are over!' young Jim said gleefully. 'You've lost your turn.'

'Daddy?' Fergus stooped to squat beside his father, who puffed tranquilly on his cigarette, then knocked the ash off with his index finger. 'Listen, Daddy,' Fergus said. 'Isn't helping other people one of the ways in which we can save our souls?'

'Our Blessed Lord,' his father began, bowing his head devotionally at mention of the Holy Name, 'put it as follows in the

Scriptures. "As you would, said Christ, that men should do to you, do you also to them in like manner." '

'Then help me!'

'But, Fergus, we've always tried to help you,' his mother said. 'Both your father and I scrimped and saved so that you children would have the benefit of a university education.'

'That's quite true, Julia,' his Aunt Mary agreed. 'And, goodness knows, without a university education, a person does not get very far nowadays.'

'There was nothing we wouldn't do for you children,' his mother said. 'Sometimes I ask myself what use it was, all the sacrifices we made, the things we denied ourselves, the clothes I didn't buy myself, the holidays we never took. So many things! Things we never mentioned to you, because we didn't want you to feel badly about it.'

The mob, approaching, was close enough to be heard, a wave of sound preceding it, a scramble of imprecations and threats, indecipherable, as though spoken in some subhuman tongue. Fergus, looking anxiously in the direction of this danger, saw that some of those in the front ranks carried sticks and slats of wood picked up from the beach wrack. Some yards ahead of the mob, half-running, stumbling, still trying to preserve lost modesty by pulling her sweater down over her plump white thighs, the girl he could not remember came, panting, eyeing Fergus plaintively, as though willing him to save her. Turning from this sight, Fergus gripped his mother by the wrist, squeezing so tightly that his mother grimaced with pain.

'Listen to me, Mama, listen! Why do you never *listen* to anything I say? I'm not talking about your past sacrifices, yes, thanks very much for all you did, thanks a million! But now, I'm asking you for *information!* Tell me what it is I'm supposed to have done with that girl?'

'Girls, girls,' his mother said, beginning to laugh. 'I know you children make fun of me for saying this, but it's true, all the same. You can have lots of girls, but you'll only have one mother. A boy's best friend is his mother.'

'Daddy, for God's sake!' Fergus said, turning to his father. 'Look at that mob. Do you want to see me killed?'

162

'Well, I must say,' Dr Fadden, stroking his moustache, winked at Fergus's mother. 'Lord help me if I'd ever spoken to *my* father in that tone of voice.'

'You wouldn't have done it twice, I can promise you that!' Fergus's mother agreed.

Below, on the beach, the mob halted. The girl, stumbling, kept running towards Fergus. On the fringes of the mob, people bent down, searching, picking up debris. Others were already hurling sticks and stones in the direction of the running girl, these missiles kicking up little plumes of sand around her as she continued on up towards the picnic site. Dr Fadden, drawing on his cigarette, peered down at the girl. 'Hmm,' said he, blowing out a thick puff of smoke. 'If there's one thing I don't understand about the present generation, it's that they seem to want everything to be done for them.'

'Exactly!' his mother said. 'I mean, they have absolutely no ambition.'

'Well, the world isn't run just to suit them. They'll find that out soon enough.'

'And, of course,' said his mother, 'it's very easy to make fun of older people. They're very good at that. But, we'll see how they do when their turn comes.'

The girl, hit in the back by a heavy piece of driftwood, fell in the sand, panting, her hair in her eyes. The mob, as though on signal, ceased throwing sticks and began to advance on her.

'Anyway, we did our best,' Dr Fadden said. 'We tried to teach them some manners and give them a good education. The rest is up to them.'

The girl, getting to her feet again, looked back at the mob, and then, in a final burst of energy, ran the last twenty yards towards the picnic site. Panting, she stopped in front of Fergus, catching hold of his arm. 'Hurry!' she said. 'Please! Come on?'

'Daddy!' Fergus said. 'Look at this girl. If you won't help me, won't you help her?'

'That lassie,' said his father, 'would be well advised to cover herself up. There are children present. Disgraceful!'

'I can see her bare bum,' Jim whispered, giggling.

'You're a dirty wee thing!' Maeve said to Jim. 'But she's worse, going around like that.'

The unknown girl tugged again at Fergus's arm. 'Please! We've got to get away!' and then, seeing him hesitate, cried impatiently, 'Don't be childish. You *know* they're no help!' And so, taking her hand in his, he turned abruptly from his family and began to run along the sands, he and the girl easily outdistancing the mob, which advanced as far as the picnic ground and then came to a stop, as though unaware that its quarry had run off. Looking back, seeing this, Fergus for the first time began to hope. And when he and the unknown girl, veering to the right, ran up into a gully between the sand dunes, emerging in a desolate tract of bushes and beach grass, he slowed to a walk and looked at her with gratitude and affection. 'We've dodged them,' he said. 'At least, I think so.'

'I seem to have caused you so much trouble, Fergus.'

'No. But why couldn't you have told me where it was we met?'

'You mean you really don't remember?'

'I don't.' He looked at her bare thighs; he tried not to, but couldn't help himself. 'Please?' he said. 'Give me a clue?'

'I can't.'

'Why not?'

'Think about it, Fergus. If you don't remember me, you don't remember me.'

'My family told me that you and I did something pleasant, something that helped you. Does that sound right?'

'It's a funny way of putting it,' the girl said. 'But I suppose, in a way, you could say it's true.'

'You're good-looking. Did I ever make a pass at you?'

She smiled but did not answer. He looked back at the gully. There was no sign of the mob. He went to her, took her in his arms, and tried to kiss her. But she drew back, uncomfortable and embarrassed. 'I'm sorry,' he said, and released her.

'That's all right.'

'I mean, I just wondered if there was something between us once. But, I guess not. You were married to – Tom. You were never involved with me.'

She smiled sadly, he thought, and then gave a small, theatrical sigh, and that sigh, seemingly inconsequential, was the thing he remembered. 'Wait!' he said. 'Now I know. We dated each other before you knew Tom. Right?'

'Of course.'

'Tom Bairstow. An Australian. Came to work on the *Long Island Gazette* about eight months after I did. You were Johannson's secretary. Elaine Rosen!'

She smiled.

'Tom succeeded me as editor, when I went to New York. And you and he got married.'

'Thanks to you,' she said. 'You were our Dan Cupid, Tom used to say. You introduced us, you persuaded me to go on a date with him, and later, you made peace between us when we had our big blow-up.'

'And I was best man at your wedding,' Fergus said. 'That crazy minister at the Unitarian Church in Riverhampton.'

'With his red silk waistcoat!'

'And he kissed the groom!'

He laughed and she laughed. 'And then Tom and I went to live in Australia. And three years ago, when we visited New York, we tried to look you up. But we missed you. I wrote to you about it.'

'Of course!'

Smiling at her in the moonlight, she smiling at him. A dry Santa Ana wind from the desert crackled across this tract of beach grass. A tumbleweed, rolling over and over like some giant child's toy, came in fitful, dragging gusts across the grass, catching, stopping, held against Fergus's legs. He kicked it free. 'Then why?' he asked. 'I mean, what in God's name were those people going on about, back there?'

'I don't know. But then, I don't know how you forgot us. I suppose you meant more to us than we meant to you. We were very fond of you, Fergus.'

'But those people should be told that,' he said. 'Look what they did to you! My God!' Anger, like a drunkenness, swelled in his head as he stared at her cut face and torn clothes, felt the pain of their sneak blows on his own shoulders and neck. 'Those foul-minded bastards! Let's find them and tell them a few home truths!'

'You go,' she said. 'Look, I don't even have a skirt on.'

'But that's what I mean! They shouldn't be allowed to get away with this. Come on. Let's find them!'

She nodded with the air of someone accepting a foolish decision, and he took her hand, turning towards the gully. There was no sign of the mob. Ploughing heavily in the soft sand as they left the tract of beach grass, they went down between the moonlit, enchanted sandbanks as though entering some Sahara at night. Anger quickened his step, but she seemed to hold back. 'You go ahead,' she said. 'I'll catch up.'

'I'll wait for you.'

'No. Hurry. You may miss them.'

He nodded, and releasing her hand, began to run, going down towards the beach. As he came out onto the shore, meeting the slow crash of breakers, the moonlight taut as a ghost tarpaulin on the flat sands, he looked around but at first could not see the mob. Then, over at Point Dume, a quarter of a mile away, he saw a dark mass moving towards the headland, going away from him, moving quickly, a desert caravan. 'Hey?' he heard himself call.

'Hey?' called a blurred echo.

'Come back here!'

'Back here.'

He watched, heavy with anger and frustration as the mass moved on, now seeming less like a desert caravan than a collection of small beach creatures, scurrying sandpipers, perhaps, or now, becoming smaller as he watched, a dark swarm of insects, smaller, smaller, then, at last, disappearing around the headland of Point Dume. He turned to Elaine Rosen, but she was nowhere in sight. He looked back up the gully. It was deserted. 'Elaine?' he called. 'Elaine, where are you?' But this time there was not even an echo of his voice. High above him on the distant bluffs, a heavy truck, night-hauling down Pacific Coast Highway, went by with an earthquake rumble. 'Elaine?' he called again, but knew his shout was rhetorical. He was alone.

Alone, he turned in the direction of the house, and at once,

pain overcame him, a pain so intense it seemed as though someone had driven a large knife into his chest. He went down on his
knees, bending over, the moonlight going black. Then, his sight
clearing, he stared at the sands, alone, in terrible, lancing pain,
sweat running in cold little rivers down his face, dripping off his
nose and chin. He thought to get to the house, wake Dani, get
to a hospital. He tried to stand, but the pain made his head whirl.
Breathing harshly, he looked, first right, then left. He saw lights
above him at the edge of the beach. A car's headlights.

He saw the car. It was parked on the small beach road which
led up to the main highway. Bullet-nosed, grey, with a black canvas top, it was the old Morris Minor his father had driven for a
dozen years. The pride of Nuffield Motors in pre-war days, it now
stood, solitary and antique, on this lonely beach road, engine
turning over, long running board a-tremble, great brass headlamps sending cones of yellow light down the moon-silvered road,
its rakish mudguards arched like horns over the narrow old-
fashioned tyres. The trunk of the car was open, and Maeve, Aunt
Mary, and Kathleen were loading wicker picnic baskets into it.
Jim and his mother stood on the side of the road, facing each
other, advancing and retreating in a parody minuet as they folded
and refolded the large picnic tablecloth. Fergus looked around
for his father, but though the engine was running, no one was at
the wheel of the car. His father was below on the sands, the last
person at the picnic site, kneeling on one knee, carefully dismant-
ling the primus stove. The sands had been raked over; there was
no litter. Dr Fadden abhorred a mess. Careful and precise, he
placed each component of the dismantled portable stove into an
old-fashioned black leather medical bag which he kept for this
purpose. As Fergus watched, Dr Fadden, completing his task,
stood up, snapped the bag shut, dusted grains of sand from his
cream flannel trousers, then turned and came towards Fergus,
adjusting his pince-nez spectacles, the better to peer down at
him.

'Ah,' said Dr Fadden. 'There you are. I wondered where you'd
got to.'

Above, on the beach road, the Klaxon horn of the old car
sounded, loud and urgent. Dr Fadden, without looking back,

waved his hand, acknowledging the summons. 'Ready?' he asked Fergus. 'Time to go, isn't it?'

The knife of pain cut into Fergus's chest. He opened his mouth but could not speak. Up at the road, the ghostly old car stood in the moonlight, its engine running. His father waited, peering down at him professionally over the half-moons of his spectacles. If only I can get up and walk away, Fergus thought. He willed himself to stand. He willed himself, and stood, the pain so intense that he lost his vision, standing, swaying blind, as the pain fell on him like a wave. It receded. He heard his breathing, stertorous, loud as a tearing rag, a sound like Aunt Mary on her deathbed, long ago.

'Yes,' said Dr Fadden, nodding in confirmation. 'You've just had a heart attack.'

And waited. And watched.

I will turn away, Fergus told himself. I will get up to the house. He turned and paced two dragging steps in that direction. Then stopped, gasping, his breathing tight. His father came alongside him, stretched out his hand, and took hold of his wrist. His father, in a remembered gesture, produced a gold half-hunter watch from his trouser pocket and studied its dial, taking Fergus's pulse.

Fergus stood, gasping for breath. His father let go of his wrist and repocketed the watch, professionally discreet. He made no comment. With all his will, Fergus raised his head, and, his vision clouding, looked towards the house. He walked a step, gasped in pain, then made a second step. The pain seemed to ease. A third step. A fourth. The pain seemed to be leaving him. But he became aware that, again, his father had followed him. He turned.

They stood in the moonlight, staring at each other. Then, at last, Dr Fadden removed his spectacles from the bridge of his nose and gave the small, professional, prefatory cough Fergus remembered so well. 'Exercise is important,' Dr Fadden said. 'And diet. But don't overdo it. Moderation in all things.' He smiled at Fergus, and reaching out, patted his shoulder in a friendly manner. 'Tell you what. Why don't you just walk me as far as the car?'

The pain seemed to have gone. His face was wet. He took a

deep breath and smiled at his father. 'Of course. Would you like me to carry your bag?'

'No, no, this old bag fits me like a glove by now,' his father said. Together, slowly, they began to trudge across the sands. 'Yes, many's the year I carried it around on my house calls. By the way. Did you get your business settled, about that girl?'

'Yes, I remembered. I was best man at her wedding.'

'I told your mother it would come to you. It's amazing what a person can remember if he puts his mind to it.'

'It's amazing what we forget.'

'No, no,' his father said testily, as though Fergus had given a stupid answer to some school question. 'Forgetting's not the problem. There are things we'd rather forget. All of us. But we can't, you see.'

Fergus nodded. They had come to the beach road, where the other members of the family waited, sitting in the car. Dr Fadden laid down the black medical bag on the shoulder of the road and turned to Fergus as though to shake hands. 'Well,' he said, 'take care of yourself, hmm?'

Fergus stared at his father, then at the old car, the glaring yellow headlamps, the moonlit passengers inside. The pain had gone. His heart beat steadily. His father also looked in the direction of the waiting car. 'Ah,' said Dr Fadden. 'That reminds me. Let's just, let's take a little stroll down this way. There was something you wanted to ask me, wasn't there?' He took Fergus by the arm affectionately, smiling at him. 'Let me guess. You're wondering where we're off to now, in the car. Hmm?'

Fergus was silent.

'I mean,' his father said, 'what are we? Are we just a figment of your memory?'

Fergus said nothing.

'Hmm,' said his father. 'How can I put it?' He linked Fergus close and turned him around, walking him back down towards the sea. 'You know the old medical joke. This world is a matter of life and death. Some truth in that, as you'll agree, after what you've just been through. Do you understand, Fergus? I'm trying to give you an honest answer.'

'I'm not sure,' Fergus said. 'What *is* the answer?'

'Hmm.' His father stopped and looked up at the sky, pondering. Moonlight made silver slices of the lenses of his spectacles. His moustache trembled as he exhaled. 'Look,' his father said. 'We have to live and die here. Do you follow me?'

'Then you admit there's no afterlife?'

His father glanced covertly at the waiting car. He wrinkled his nose, causing his pince-nez spectacles to drop, spinning on their black silk ribbon. He ducked his head close to Fergus and whispered, 'Supposing I were to describe another world to you? Would you believe me? It wouldn't have any reality for you, would it?'

'I don't know. It might.'

'But how could it, Fergus? It would be someplace you'd never been, someplace so different you couldn't even imagine it. Just hearsay evidence.'

'Look,' Fergus said. 'If you're trying to tell me what I think you are, then don't you realize that your whole life was a farce? All the things you taught us, the things you believed in, your prayers, going to Mass and Confession and Holy Communion, your devotion to Our Lady, the whole thing! Your obedience to the rules of the church, the ten commandments, mortal sins, plenary indulgences, the lot! Just think of it! A sham, a fraud, a complete waste of time!'

'But we're not talking about me, Fergus, we're talking about you. Faith and belief, yes, I had those things in my life. We're talking about you!'

He stared at Fergus. 'Don't you see? If you have not found a meaning, then your life is meaningless.'

Fergus shivered. He felt cold. As though a last word had been said, his father turned away, moving off with his characteristic brisk walk, striding up to the beach road and the waiting motorcar. A sudden wind whipped the stalks of beach grass, sending a thin skirt of sand off the beach, to move like a low-lying fog along the concrete surface of the beach road as his father, at the shoulder of the road, picked up his black medical bag and went towards the waiting car. The Morris Minor stood, hood a-tremble, mudguards quivering, headlamps yellow-bright in the moonlight, waiting to drive off to some other, inconceivable world, a world which, his father said, would have no reality for the likes of him. The family sat in the car; his mother, Aunt Mary, Kathleen, Maeve, and Jim, all waiting. His father reached the car and went around, opening the front door, putting in his bag, then, pausing, put on his white panama hat. His father did not look back at the beach, and Fergus could not see if the others, inside the car, were looking out. It was not their move; it was his.

And suddenly, knowing this, Fergus raised his arm and waved, releasing them. His father looked up, saw the good-bye wave, and, grateful, raised his old white hat in salute. His father got into the car; the engine shuddered, the gears engaged, the old car jerked forward, spasmodic, in shaky acceleration, and now, from the opened car windows, hands waved, the family saying good-bye as the car, gathering speed, swung grandly around a curve, disappearing, then reappearing, its bright headlamps swivelling, spiralling its progress towards the main road. At the road junction it paused, elderly and out-of-date on Pacific Coast Highway, and then with a clashing of gears and a whine of acceleration, it was gone.

In the east, dawn came up. Breakers slammed on the morning shore, monotonous as a heartbeat. He walked towards the house.

More about Penguins
and Pelicans

Penguinews, which appears every month, contains details of all the new books issued by Penguins as they are published. From time to time it is supplemented by *Penguins in Print*, which is our complete list of almost 5,000 titles.

A specimen copy of *Penguinews* will be sent to you free on request. Please write to Dept EP, Penguin Books Ltd, Harmondsworth, Middlesex, for your copy.

In the U.S.A.: For a complete list of books available from Penguins in the United States write to Dept CS, Penguin Books, 625 Madison Avenue, New York, New York 10022.

In Canada: For a complete list of books available from Penguins in Canada write to Penguin Books Canada Ltd, 2801 John Street, Markham, Ontario L3R 1B4.

The Hothouse by the East River

Muriel Spark

There's something eerie about Elsa – something more than madness. Psychoanalysis achieves nothing.

One by one her husband, her children, her analyst begin to notice: Elsa's shadow falls in the wrong direction. Hour after hour she sits in the oven-hot apartment high up above the East river, seeing things. And her shadow falls towards the light.

Not to Disturb

A storm rages round the towers of the big house near Geneva. Behind the locked doors of the library, the Baron, the Baroness and their handsome young secretary are not to be disturbed. In the attic, the Baron's lunatic brother howls and hurls plates at his keeper.

But in the staff quarters, all is under control: the servants make their own, highly lucrative, preparations for the tragedy.

The night is long, but morning will bring a *crime passionel* of outstanding attraction and endless possibilities.

Muriel Spark has created a world in her own idiom – bizarre, gruesome and brilliantly funny.

V. S. Naipaul

'It is time . . . for him to be quite simply recognized as this country's most talented and promising young writer' – Anthony Powell in the *Daily Telegraph*

The Mimic Men

Living in a run-down London suburb, Ralph Singh, a disgraced colonial minister exiled from the Caribbean island of his birth, is writing his biography. When he comes to politics he finds himself caught up in the upheaval of empire, in the turmoil of too-large events which move too fast.

A House for Mr Biswas

Mohun Biswas wants success, a house and a portion of land of his own. As he moves from job to job, acquiring a wife and four children, the odds against him lengthen and his ambition becomes more remote.

The Mystic Masseur

Ganesh, who cured the Woman Who Couldn't Eat and the Man Who Made Love to His Bicycle, becomes involved in a local scandal. But he manages to keep some surprises in reserve . . .

The Suffrage of Elvira

'I promising you,' said Mrs Baksh of the Elvira district election in Trinidad, 'for all it began sweet sweet, it going to end damn sour.'

Further titles by V. S. Naipaul from Penguins include:

In a Free State
Mr Stone and the Knights Companion
Miguel Street
The Loss of El Dorado